THE LEGENDARY WEAVER

Abimbola Alao

Illustrations
By
Sameo Ogunsoa.

Lampo Press
www.lampoeducation.co.uk

Book & CD

First published in Great Britain in 2003 by Lampo Press
P O Box 185
Woolwell
Plymouth
PL6 7ZN

Website: www.lampoeducation.co.uk
E-mail: info@lampoeducation.co.uk

British Library Cataloguing in Publication Data
A catalogue record for this book is available from the British Library

ISBN 0-9546255-0-1

Printed in Great Britain by E.J. Rickard Ltd., Plymouth. (01752) 660955

"Abimbola has woven magic into this simple tale of love and locks. Kike, our young heroine has a life changing experience when she became deaf; heralding the start of an exciting spiritual journey. Set in Aje, a small village in Nigeria, the tale is bursting with magical stories and is accompanied on CD with traditional songs from West Africa. 'The Legendary Weaver' touches the heart and nourishes the soul."

Fiona Evans Roots Coordinator, BBC Radio Devon.

"Abimbola Alao is known to many across Devon for her storytelling and educational work. However, she makes her publishing debut with 'The Legendary Weaver,' the story of an African girl's battle with disability. Even though the book is easy to follow, it is also sophisticated in its message of hope over adversity.

Abimbola's skill as a tale-teller is evident from the off. Like all the best novelists, you cannot tear your eyes from the page. Also, her vivid descriptions of African life will remain in your mind's eye perfectly as you leaf through this work."

Evening Herald

"I found 'The Legendary Weaver,' a good resource book even for pre-schoolers. It is wonderful to show the children, first hand, how people in other parts of the world tell stories, sing, play and dance. The short stories, in the book, for example, *'Kulumbu Yeye,'* can be read to pre-school and foundation stage children, and the CD of African songs that comes with the book makes the storytelling interactive. It also helps us to introduce children to the rich West African culture of call and response storytelling."

Sue Shapley, Play leader and Administrator,
Woolwell Under Fives Pre-school

DEDICATION

In loving memory of my grandmother,
Mama Rachel Omotoso,
who departed this world on the 21st of June, 2003.

PROLOGUE

I REMEMBER the day clearly. I was about ten years old and it was a Saturday. I had gone to my grandmother to have my hair plaited in readiness for school.

My grandma, as usual, had thought of a style before I arrived, and soon she began, painstakingly and meticulously, to carve out an intricate design in my hair. At school the following week, I nearly got my neck twisted out of joint because my teachers and classmates couldn't stop admiring the clever pattern.

'So what's this style called?' asked Mrs Omole, the class-two teacher.

'Aja n'loso,' I beamed.

'Stooping dog! Who plaited it for you?'

'My grandmother.'

'How smart!' she exclaimed. 'See the way she's sewn the top bit that represents the dog's ear, making it look like the real thing.'

'And what are these knotted bits?' Mrs Edonmi, who taught kindergarten, chipped in.

'Those are meant to be the dog's paws,' I answered proudly.

That was it. After this incident, I was thrown into the limelight because of the unusual and complex styles that my grandmother plaited for me weekly. Some of the styles were so convoluted – for example *Oju Ekun*, 'eye of the tiger' – that not even the self-acclaimed expert braiders could figure it out. I was quite pleased with my new-found fame. Luckily, I had no competitor, as most other girls wore simple, straightforward styles.

As time went on, I became more and more fascinated by this awesome art and I began to wonder how African braiding, especially cornrow design, was invented.

One day, I asked my grandmother the question that was bugging me. 'Mama, who invented cornrow braids?'

She heaved a sigh, smiled and said, 'I asked my mother this same question many years ago, and she told me an intriguing story about the origin of the craft. I guess it's my turn to be the storyteller.'

'Will you share the story with me today?' I beseeched.

'Of course,' Grandma answered. 'You see, Cornrow design, which is a unique type of hair braiding, was discovered many years ago. My mother told me an amazing story about its invention when I was a little girl, so now; I too will narrate it to you. However, I must warn you that it is a very long story of sadness, hope deferred, bravery, and joy at dawn.'

I nodded; not exactly sure I understood what all those big words had to do with hair braiding. However, I couldn't wait to find out. My grandmother then took me back in time to Aje, an ancient village, in the southern part of Nigeria, in West Africa, where a girl called Kike lived her life, not knowing she would one day make history.

Chapter 1

THE DREADED FEVER

IT was a very cloudy day and it had started to rain. As the drizzles gradually turned to heavy downpour, thunder and lightning began to exchange occasional glances, forcing the earth beneath them to tremble and lighten up. Aduni was getting ready to go to the market when her daughter came into her room, yawning widely.

'I feel tired,' she said, looking worn out.

Aduni paused for a moment, to observe her daughter. 'You do look tired, and I'll suggest you don't come with me to the market today. Why don't you go back to bed? Maybe you've had a lot of mosquito bites. The rainy season brings with it those dreadful insects. When I come back, I'll make you some herb tea.'

'Okay, Mother,' said Kike reluctantly.

'I think a rest will do you good. I'll come straight home as soon as I finish work.' Aduni patted her daughter's head affectionately.

Aduni had her own small business, selling batiks in the local market, and Kike went with her to help, as well as learn the trade.

1

That morning, she was a bit reluctant to leave her daughter alone at home. Kike was Aduni and Jakobu's only child and with Jakobu away, it was not easy. His family did not see much of him, because their kingdom, Owu, was experiencing a lot of trouble from the Borgu Empire in the Northern part of Nigeria. Soldiers from all the villages and towns in the kingdom were drafted to war. Kike longed for her father to stay home more, and many times she complained about his long absence.

'Why can't he be like other fathers?' she would ask her mum. 'It doesn't feel like I have a father. He just appears like a stranger and before I get to know him or befriend him he is gone.'

'Don't say things like that,' Aduni often rebuked her. 'Your father is a patriotic Owu man who is serving his kingdom in this time of crisis. You don't know how hard these soldiers have to fight to save us from being carted away as slaves by the Borgus. They are heroes risking their lives for us and the least we can do is be grateful.'

When Kike realised how much her mum hurt whenever she complained about her father's long absence, she decided to stop, even though she was sad.

That morning, after her mum had gone to work, Kike went back to bed, but she could not sleep, because she felt so uncomfortable.

'Oh, my head,' she groaned, rolling from side to side. She could feel it throbbing as if a mortar and pestle had been placed on her crown and someone was pounding yam on it. Suddenly she began to feel sick. She quickly got out of bed, barely making it to the back yard before vomiting all over the floor. She tried to make herself stop, but she could not hold it back; it kept gushing out of her mouth.

Even when she got to the back yard, she still continued to throw up, but not as much as she did indoors. She then heard someone calling from a distance:

'Kike! Kike! Are you all right?'

It was Tito, the next-door neighbour. She jumped over the low shrubs that separated the two houses, and ran to where Kike was.

'Oh no, it's the chatterbox! I'll just pretend there is nothing wrong with me,' Kike murmured.

By now Tito was standing by her, looking worried. 'What's the matter? Are you ill, where's your mother?'

'She's gone to the market,' Kike managed. She was still feeling sick.

Tito rushed into the kitchen, grabbed a cup and took some water from a tank nearby. Then she sprinkled some on Kike's face, before urging her to drink some.

'How could your mother have left you alone in the house and not even tell me you are ill?' said Tito angrily. 'I would have brought you over to my house to keep an eye on you. Why do people behave like this – does she think I'm not capable of looking after you?'

She went on and on for the next five minutes.

I can see why people call this woman talkative, thought Kike. One of the villagers once said she could talk non-stop for ten days. 'I'm fine now,' Kike cut in rudely to get the woman off her back. 'It's just that I ate too much late last night and it didn't digest properly.'

'Poor child, you don't look okay to me. Get up so I can check your belly.'

Kike got up with a lot of difficulty because she was aching all over. Tito helped her up and pressed her stomach so hard it hurt.

'Ouch!' she whined in pain.

'You're very ill, and you're going to stay with me until your mother comes back from the market,' Tito said emphatically.

'Oh no – um - I mean, thank you but I prefer to lie down in my own bed,' Kike pleaded. The thought of staying with Tito all day sent chills down her spine.

'Not in the state you're in, my dear child. You're coming with me, and that is Final!' Tito always refers to Kike as 'my dear child.' This is a common practice in many African countries. Adults look after children in their neighbourhood as they would their own, especially in the absence of the children's real parents.

Tito lifted Kike up like a tiny toddler and flipped her across her broad shoulder.

Wow! no one has carried me like this for ages. This woman is so strong, thought Kike as she journeyed on her neighbour's huge shoulder.

Tito carried Kike to her house and carefully placed her on an old wooden bed in one of the rooms. 'Now lie down here, I'll see if I have some dogoyaro left in the house to make you some herbal tea,' said Tito.

'Please, I don't want dogoyaro. It makes me sick,' Kike pleaded. She had never liked the bitter herb, which is still used in Africa today as anti-malaria medicine. 'I'll take anything but that horrible stuff,' she continued pleading.

'All right, I'll leave it for now, but if you get any worse, I will have to give it to you. Take some rest now and if you need anything just call me. I'll be out in the yard washing clothes.' Tito does *agbafo* (launderette). Unfortunately, she did not get paid much; hence she took on a lot of laundry jobs. She had seven children, which included a set of twins. Her husband was also a soldier; hence he too was away at the time.

'Don't worry about me' Kike said. 'All I need is a good sleep and I'll be fine.' She faked a yawn, covered her body with the cloth her neighbour gave her and closed her eyes as if ready to sleep.

'Poor child,' Tito sympathised on her way out to resume her washing.

When she had gone, Kike opened her eyes and managed to look around the room. It was a bit dark because the only window there was tiny and high up. The whole place smelled of palm oil and black soap and the cobwebs that hung on the ceiling made the room feel eerie.

'This room reminds me of Ma Moji's house. I wonder what has happened to that wicked woman,' Kike whispered. 'It's been a while since my mum sent me to buy kola nut from her. Not since the day she called me a witch.' As Kike began to doze, she recalled the incident.

That day, Ma Moji's dog barked ferociously at her and even tugged on her skirt. In anger, Kike kicked the dog off and Ma Moji came charging like a blood-thirsty lion. Anyone would have thought she was about to have a go at another adult. Shamelessly, she began to heap abusive words on Kike.

'Carry your bad luck away from my house, you evil witch,' she shouted. 'Do you want to kill my dog like you killed the other children that your mother should have given birth to?'

Kike was taken aback and began to cry. She turned round and ran all the way home. Her mother, who was indoors, rushed out when she heard her daughter's loud wailing.

'My jewel, what is the matter?' she enquired, running halfway down the front yard to meet her daughter.

'It's Ma Moji. She…she…she called me a witch and she said I killed the other children that you could have had. I killed no one…I haven't killed anyone,' Kike sobbed.

Aduni gently led her daughter indoors from the prying eyes of the neighbours. 'Now calm down and tell me what happened.' She listened in anger to the shocking story her daughter narrated to her. When Kike finished, Aduni got up and paced up and down the room, head bowed and deep in thought. Then she straightened up and looked straight into her daughter's eyes.

'Stay here and don't go out,' she instructed. She got a strip of cloth from a nearby chair, and irately tied it round her waist.

Aduni was fuming. Her eyes were dilating and turning red by the minute. Her lips were curled up towards her nose like that of a cheeky baboon. She must have hissed a dozen times before she finally stormed out of her house towards Ma Moji's. Kike was frightened. She had never seen her mother in that mood before. Aduni was naturally gentle and soft spoken. Kike knew there was going to be trouble.

Oto the palm wine taper was coming home from work. He met Aduni just outside her house. 'Aduni *omo* Sonibare *ara o le bi*?' he called in greeting. By this he meant 'Aduni the daughter of Sonibare, how are you?' He hadn't yet got over his infatuation for the attractive woman.

Aduni was not in the mood for good-natured remarks, so she stormed past the old man like a whirlwind.

This is most unlike her, thought Oto. Aduni is one of the most respectful individuals in this village. For her not to greet me or not to respond to my greeting means something is terribly wrong. He decided to go after her and find out what was happening. Unfortunately, he could not keep up with her. He called after her, but when he got no response, he decided to give up.

'I have had a busy day,' he thought to himself, before turning back to go to his own house. 'I don't need to trouble myself by poking my nose into other people's affairs. I think I should make my way home, eat some pounded yam and drench it with a sizeable calabash of palm wine.' The thought of this brought a smile to the face of the pot-bellied old man.

One of Ma Moji's neighbours saw Aduni coming, and she quickly alerted her. Cowardly, Ma Moji ran out through her back door and disappeared into the bush.

'It's not that I am weak or fearful,' she mumbled, trying to convince herself that she had made a wise move. 'Our elders say that in order to avoid an encounter with evil, let your feet be the medicine.' In other words, run for dear life when faced with trouble or danger. With this she ran as fast as she could.

Aduni arrived to an empty house. No one knew where Ma Moji had gone. Aduni searched Ma Moji's house, room by room, but could not find her. Then she came out to the front yard where neighbours had gathered, eagerly waiting to see what was going to happen.

'Tell that spineless coward I'll pay her another visit,' she said to one of the neighbours. 'When I come back for her, I'll show her what a real witch can do. She hasn't seen one yet. By the time I finish with her, she'll have no teeth left in her mouth and she will learn a lesson or two about how to bridle her dirty old tongue.' By now Aduni was holding out her fist in rage. She hissed and spat indignantly as she stormed out of the place.

Kike was anxiously waiting for her mum by the front door. 'Mother, where did you go?' she cried.

'Don't you worry about that!' Aduni replied sharply, frustrated that she was unable to vent her anger on Ma Moji. 'Listen to me, child, you are not a witch and you have not killed anyone. You are the only child God has given to your father and me, and we could not have asked for a better gift. That is why we decided to call you Kikelomo, which, as you know means, a child to be pampered. You are our precious child.'

As Kike recalled her mum's comforting words, she began to smile and before long she drifted off to sleep. She dreamt that she went to the brook to wash her clothes and she saw Ma Moji there. Ma Moji suddenly turned into a killer spider and was running after her. Kike ran until she became breathless and could go no further and she fell flat on her face. In the dream, she got up, determined that she would not allow the spider to kill her, so she got hold of a large stick and began to hit the spider's head, shouting, 'You cannot kill me, you dirty old witch. Be gone! Be gone!'

'Calm down! Calm down! 'Shush, stop it,' were the words that roused Kike from her nightmares. She woke up to find her mother bending over her.

'Where am I?' she asked.

'You are safe at home, my jewel,' reassured Aduni. 'Are you feeling better now?'

'Yes, I am, thank you, mother. Did you pick me up from our neighbour's house?'

'Yes, I came back from the market a few minutes ago, and I was alarmed when I didn't see you. I quickly went over to Tito's house to ask if she'd seen you and she told me all that happened. She also reprimanded me for leaving you alone at home and not asking her to look after you. You were sleeping peacefully when she took me to the room where you were. Luckily, her brother Kosoko was visiting, so he helped me carry you back home. I am so sorry, my angel. If I knew you were ill, I would have stayed at home with you. I thought you were just tired.'

'Mother, I was not very poorly when you left for the market this morning. I know you would not have left me alone at home if you knew I would be sick,' said Kike, trying to comfort her mother.

'Tomorrow, I'll ask Ewedara, the village doctor to come and have a look at you, I don't want to take any chances,' said her mum.

Chapter 2

WELCOME BACK!

A S usual, Aduni was the first to wake up the following morning. She began to tidy up the house and on her way to the back yard she paused by her daughter's bedroom door to see if she had woken up.

'Kike, are you up? How is your headache, are you feeling better?' Aduni called.

'Ugh! My head hurts badly,' moaned Kike as she rolled out of bed. 'Mother, please come, I can't see very well.'

Aduni immediately dropped the pile of clothes she was carrying and hurried to her daughter. What is the matter?' she enquired.

'My head ached throughout the night and as I got out of bed, everywhere went black and I feel light-headed.'

'Sit back in bed and I'll check you over.' Oh, see how hot your body is!' exclaimed Aduni. She made a dash for the back yard, and came back with a bowl of water and a flannel. She dipped the flannel in the cold water and dabbed Kike's temple with it. The chill was a rude shock to her body and she began to shake like a reed on a windy day.

'It's too cold,' she protested, trying to hold her mother's hands off her head.

'I know, my beauty, but it'll keep your temperature down.'

'Oh, my head, my neck, I feel choked,' cried Kike groaning in pain.

'I think I'll call Ewedara to come and see you,' said Aduni, who was now very worried. She went out of the room towards the back yard and Kike could hear her calling one of the twins next door.

'Taiwo! Taiwo!'

Taiwo came as fast as he could.

'Kindly rush down to Ewedara the village doctor and tell him he should please come quickly,' said Aduni. 'It's Kike, she is very ill. Then she added, 'Thank you, my child, if you come back on time, I'll give you something nice.'

Taiwo beamed with joy at the thought of getting a present, so he quickly went to tell his mum that Aduni had sent him on an errand.

'Go get a shirt; you are not planning to go out bare-chested, are you?'

'Mother, it's too hot – I'm going to run to and fro, hence I can't catch cold.' He then moved his right foot forward as if ready to do a relay race, and shot off like lightning.

Ewedara lived about a mile away from Kike's house, but he came as soon as he got Aduni's message. The old man was about seventy-eight years old, but had the physique of a forty-five-year-old man. Tall and hefty, with a broad chest, he carried himself with dignity. In his youth, he was a renowned boxer. He began his career as an herbalist at the age of fifty, after the death of his father and he became a reputable and well-respected medicine man in the region.

People said he could diagnose any ailment and he had a cure for most of them. He was a bit of a show-off too, because Kike once heard him boasting that he had brought ten dead people back to life. When Kike asked her father if it was true, Jakobu shrugged and said, 'Those people had merely fainted and he brought them back to consciousness by using a type of strong herbal oil.'

'Peace be unto this house!' Ewedara called as he came into Kike's home with his apprentice, who carried a wooden box, containing various medicines.

'May peace also abide with our visitors,' Aduni answered as she hurried to the door to welcome them. Then she led the old man and his apprentice to where Kike was and briefly explained what was happening to her daughter.

Ewedara carefully examined Kike. 'Stick out your tongue for me to see,' he said, and he placed his hand under Kike's chin. He then lifted her eyelids until they hurt. 'How are you feeling now?'

'My head hurts badly and my belly aches as well.'

'Why not tell Pa Ewedara about your ears,' Aduni interrupted.

'Yes, my ears echo a lot and whenever people speak to me they sound as if they are in a cave.'

Ewedara sat up when Kike said this. He took off his cap and scratched his bald head lightly but fretfully. A frown creased his forehead. Kike could not explain the look on his face, because he looked startled and puzzled all at once. Then he spoke directly to Aduni, 'Initially I thought your daughter was suffering from malaria fever, caused by mosquito bite, but what puzzles me is why her tongue is so black, and why her ears echo. Malaria hardly affects people this way. I will speak to a colleague of mine and hear what he has to say. I'll come and give you a feedback.

Have you got dogoyaro at home?'

'Yes,' confirmed Aduni.

'Boil some and add this root to it while it is still cooking.' He handed her a brown plant, which he took out of his medicine box. 'Goodbye for now.'

'Thank you very much and give my love to your wife,' said Aduni as she escorted the doctor and his apprentice to the door.

Aduni set out to make the herb tea and an hour later she came in with a bowl of steaming dogoyaro. She handed it over to her daughter.

'Here, drink it all up.'

Kike began to frown. She hated the bitter herb.

'The smell of this repulsive drink is enough to raise the dead,' she said.

'Shut up and drink the thing!' her mother ordered. 'You heard what the doctor said. I don't think this is the time to mess around. Your health is at risk here.'

Kike took a deep breath, then she held it as she put the bowl to her lips and drank non-stop until the bowl was empty. She then belched loudly and went back to sleep.

It was getting dark, and the crickets had started their evening concert. Aduni, who had been by her daughter's bedside all day, suddenly noticed a change in her breathing. It was as if Kike was gasping for breath. Alarmed, she shook Kike to wake her up from sleep, thinking it was the way she had positioned her head. 'Change your position, Kike,' she ordered. When her daughter did not respond, she repeated, 'I said turn and change your position.'

Unfortunately, Kike could not hear her mother. She had begun to drift in and out of consciousness, as the fever had eaten its way into her system. Her body was so hot you could roast a piece of plantain on it.

Aduni jumped off her seat, grabbed her daughter with both arms and clutched her to her chest.

'Kikeeeeeee!' she screamed, but her daughter lay limp in her arms, eyes rolled up into their sockets. Somehow Aduni knew that there was no time for sentiment. The situation was a battle between life and death, and if she ever wanted to see her daughter alive, she had to do something! She laid Kike face-up on the mat and seized the bowl of water near the bed. She then began to apply cold water on her daughter's body with the flannel she had used earlier. She continued to call her name, saying, 'Hear me, my jewel; you are all I've got. You cannot leave me here alone. Please don't let my enemies mock me. You are a gift from God and I am not going to release you to death.'

With trembling hands, she continued to massage her body with the flannel and cold water, calling her name all along.

'Please, my child, answer me. Please, I beg,' she cried.

Kike lay still on the bed, her face as pale as death. Aduni by now was becoming hysterical. She began to shout at the top of her voice, 'Help me, somebody! Help!' She was yelling, jumping up and down and holding her head with both hands. Then she ran outside the house, screaming, 'Please, somebody help me. Please don't let my child die.'

It was Tito who first heard her voice. She was doing her laundry in her back yard, and she immediately left the clothes and rushed to Aduni's house.

'Aduni!' she called. 'Aduni, what is it?'

'It's my child, it is Kike, she fainted and I tried to revive her. Please help me, don't let my child die.'

'She is not going to die,' said Tito emphatically. 'Where is she?'

'In there,' said Aduni, pointing in the direction of her daughter's room.

Tito took one look at Kike and realised she had to do something fast in order to save the little girl. 'Hold yourself together, Aduni. Let me go and fetch my mother, she's skilled in this sort of thing. I don't know what to do and I don't want to waste any more time.'

She ran off and soon reappeared with a toothless, frail-looking old woman. Tito's mum, who lived directly opposite her daughter, was another powerful herbalist, known for her sound knowledge of traditional medicine. Her cracked and wrinkled skin was a tell-tale sign of a woman who had been around for a while. Tito once told her friends that her mum was about eighty years old. In spite of her age, she had the strides of a healthy fifty-year-old, even though she was bent over like the curved end of a walking stick. Every strand of hair on her head was white like pure cotton wool. She always got Yomi the barber to trim it for her.

'Where is she?' the old woman asked in a husky voice.

'In there,' said Aduni pointing to the room where Kike was. She was too frightened to go in with them.

Mama Berta, the elder, who held weekly storytelling meetings in her house, came in just then. 'I was on my way to the blacksmith, who was mending one of my looms when I heard the noise,' she said to Aduni. Then she caught sight of Tito's mother, entering Aduni's house, and she immediately guessed what must be happening. 'Let me come and help you,' she said to the old woman.

'Yes, thank you, Berta, I'm sure I'll need your assistance.' Then she turned to her daughter and said, 'Tito, please bring Aduni indoors and stay with her in the front room. Kike is going to be fine, I promise.'

She and Mama Berta hurriedly made their way to Kike's room, where they found her lying flat on her back, still and lifeless. The old woman immediately began to shake the girl vigorously, at the same time calling her name loudly, but unfortunately she got no response. She then said, 'Berta, keep the girl's body flat on the floor, while I feel her breath.' She bent down and put her face near Kike's nose. When she got up, she shook her head sadly and quickly ripped Kike's blouse open, exposing her bare chest. She

13

14

watched her chest for a while to see if there was any movement. 'Goodness and Mercy!' she yelled, she has stopped breathing!' She then held the girl's head with both her hands, and tilted it backwards.

Meanwhile, three other women had arrived to see what was happening.

'Oh my child,' Aduni wailed. 'Please don't let her die, if she dies I will kill myself,' she said, bashing her head on the wall. Tito and another woman tried to hold her down to no avail. Although, Aduni was not a big woman, the two women still found it difficult to overpower her. Every time she looked towards the room where her daughter lay, she threw herself on the concrete floor.

'Please, Aduni, don't kill yourself,' Tito begged. 'Your daughter is going to live.'

'How do you know that?' shouted Aduni, turning to face Tito as if she was going to pounce on her. Her long hair was in a terrible state as she kept pulling it. She looked like a mad woman.

Tito ignored her question and continued to calm her down. 'It's of no use, harming yourself now. You need a lot of strength to nurse Kike back to strength when she wakes up.'

'Leave me alone and let me die here and now, I see no reason why I should live.'

'Stop those negative words,' said a voice behind them. The women turned around to see Mama Berta standing by the door of the sitting-room. 'We need your cooperation if you want Kike back. Do you not know that life and death lies within your tongue? Please watch the words you utter, because you shall have whatever you say, either positive or negative.'

She moved closer to Aduni, took her by the hand and led her to the back yard and beckoned to Tito to come with them.

'Aduni,' she said, 'the situation right now is very critical. I have the belief that Kike would be resuscitated but we need your help.'

'My help?' asked Aduni, who was shaking all over.

'Yes, your help,' confirmed Mama Berta. 'I want you to refocus. I want you to close your eyes and see yourself, holding your daughter, laughing and cuddling her. I know it is difficult but, believe me, there is power in this simple action. It is called creating the impossible. I cannot explain it all to you right now, but listen, the reason why it is said that you are made in the image of God is that you have the power to create. You are now going to put this into action, by crafting in your mind's eye the positive scene that I have just described to you. The old woman and I are fighting for your daughter's life, but we need you to work with us by doing this. Can you?'

Aduni nodded even though she did not know how forming a picture in her mind could save her daughter.

'Good,' said Mama Berta. 'Now, Tito, I want you to repeat these words to Aduni: "Kike, welcome back to the land of the living."'

Tito began to say the words immediately and Mama Berta hurried back indoors. She told the other women who had gathered in the house to leave Aduni and Tito for a while. 'Kike is going to be fine,' she assured them.

One by one, they began to leave the house, and Mama Berta went back to assist the old woman, who was by now working on Kike's chest, trying to give her a kind of cardiac massage.

'I am beginning to get some response,' said the old woman. 'It is now time to use *gbekude* smelling oil.'

'What smelling oil?' asked Mama Berta, puzzled.

'I said *gbekude*!' the old woman snapped impatiently. 'I don't think we have time to hold a question and answer session here because we now need to act swiftly or this girl is gone forever. Now listen carefully to the instructions that I'm about to give you. Open my bag, which is by the door. You'll find a little green bottle in it. Open the bottle and hold it close to Kike's nose and keep it there until she sneezes.'

Mama Berta carefully took the oil out of the bag and opened it. She nearly fell backwards because of the smell. 'Ugh!' she gasped, trying to hold her breath. The oil smelt like a mixture of mint, tobacco, sulphur and garlic. It was so strong that it made her eyes water. One would have thought Mama Berta had been slicing onions as she wiped her hurting eyes and running nose.

She, however, managed to hold the bottle to Kike's nose, while calling her name at the same time

'Kike, my flower, please open your eyes. It's your friend Berta. Open your eyes, Kike, I promise to tell you beautiful stories, the type you love.'

Aduni was all the while pacing up and down the house. She struggled to keep the positive picture that Mama Berta described to her in her mind. It was the most difficult thing she'd ever done. It was much easier to plunge into grief. However, the desire to see her daughter alive was stronger than her own self-pity, so she tried very hard to visualise herself and Kike, singing and dancing together. She used the day her mother visited about two years back as an anchor, because she still remembered how happy her daughter was on that occasion. She kept this picture in her mind as she paced up and down the back yard.

Tito too was very helpful. She stood by her like a solid rock, repeating the words, 'Welcome back, Kike, welcome to the land of the living,' over and over again.

Just then Aduni heard Mama Berta calling Kike's name and because her voice was mixed with emotions, she thought all was lost. She began to wail and she was about to throw herself on the concrete floor again when Tito ran towards her and held her by the waist.

'Leave me alone before I head-butt you,' Aduni warned.

'Well, carry on then, I'd rather be maimed than sit by and watch you kill yourself,' Tito said firmly.

As Aduni struggled to free herself, she suddenly heard a loud sneeze coming from Kike's room.

'Achoo!'

She froze, trying to establish whether it was her daughter who was sneezing or someone else.

'Aaaaachooo!' Kike sneezed again. Then she slowly moved her head.

'She is here,' Mama Berta cried excitedly.

However, the old woman was not ready to share in the excitement just yet. She was very experienced and she knew her work was not completed yet. Her wrinkled face was set like a flint as she barked out more orders at Mama Berta. 'Now, move closer to her, and call out her name again, while I massage her feet.'

Mama Berta frantically began to call the little girl. 'Kike, my dear girl,' she cried, 'welcome back!'

Kike rolled over to her side and began to cry. 'Mother, where are you? It hurts. My head, my neck, my stomach, they all hurt.'

When Aduni heard her daughter's voice, she jumped and ran like a deer in the woods, into Kike's room.

'Oh my child, my child,' she cried, raising her hands towards the ceiling, tears rolling down her cheeks. 'Welcome back! Welcome to the land of the living.'

'Welcome?' Kike looked puzzled. 'Welcome from where, where did I go?'

Aduni grabbed her daughter and clutched her to her chest.

'Gently, Mother, you are hurting me, I feel hot and cold at the same time,' she said in a feeble voice. 'Please cover me up.' She was shivering uncontrollably.

'No!' shouted Aduni, 'I can't do that; your temperature will rise again. Here, take some water. What do you want to eat? You've had no food all day.'

'I don't feel like eating anything, I just want to go to the toilet.'

Aduni curtsied to the two elderly women who had helped to bring her daughter back to consciousness. 'Thank you very much,' she said, 'only God can reward you for your help. I owe you my life.'

'Give all the glory to God Almighty,' said the old woman in her usual matter-of-fact way. 'We are just his emissaries. I must hurry home now, it's getting late, and I don't see very well in the dark.'

Mama Berta gave Aduni a warm hug. 'I told you she was going to live,' she said smiling. 'Take Kike to the toilet while I clear this place up, then I too will have to go I'm afraid, but I'll come back tomorrow to see both of you.'

'I am most grateful to you both,' Aduni said to the two women again. She then took her daughter to the toilet.

Later that evening, as Aduni was putting her daughter to bed, Pa Ewedara called as promised. 'How is Kike?' he asked.

'It's not looking too good,' she replied. 'This evening, she passed out and it took a good one hour to bring her back, with the help of my neighbour's mother and Mama Berta. To be honest with you, I was torn apart.'

The old man nodded and said, 'Finish off what you are doing while I wait here in the front room. I have to talk to you.'

Aduni did not like the tone of the old man's voice. Something in it sent the chills down her spine. The hair on her neck stood up straight and her body was covered in goose pimples. She had a feeling her life was never going to be the same again. She quickly settled her daughter to bed and went back to her visitor.

The journey from Kike's room to the front yard, where Ewedara was waiting, seemed like eternity to Aduni. Her heart was pounding as if it was about to bounce off her chest. The way Aduni was walking, one would have thought a millstone was tied to her feet.

The memories came flooding back of the time she lost her only brother, when she was about twelve years old. Her brother had gone fishing with their father and in the evening of the same day he began to complain of headache and cold. By the next day he was gone. Just like that, DEAD!

No one knew what the disease was. Some said it was acute yellow fever, some said it was the cold-floor fever. Whatever it was, that was the most shocking experience of Aduni's life. The love between her and her late brother was immeasurable. Villagers thought they were twins, although he was a year older. They were of the same height and they looked very much alike.

Aduni thought she would never recover from her loss. However, the birth of Kike changed things. She was the spitting image of her late brother, and this comforted her in no small way, as she could just picture his face, every time she looked at her daughter.

Aduni's heart was troubled. Was history about to repeat itself? Was she going to lose her only daughter just like she did her only brother? 'If anything happens to my child, I will kill myself, there are no two ways about it,' she said. Then she took calculated steps to where Ewedara was, expecting the worst.

'I presume you want to tell me what you think is wrong with my child,' she announced.

'Come, my child, sit down,' the wise old man said.

'I am not sitting down, just tell me what is wrong with my daughter,' Aduni demanded harshly.

'That is exactly what I am about to do,' replied Ewedara, who was offended by the tone of Aduni's voice.

'Well?' said Aduni, looking intently at the old man.

'Um…I went to my friend Sangowanwa the herbalist, and he too was a bit puzzled when I told him about Kike, especially about the echoes she complained of and also about her tongue turning black. He feared something might be seriously wrong.'

19

'Tell me what I don't know,' Aduni thought as she listened to Ewedara. She was beginning to get impatient. 'So what did he suggest?'

'He suggested we make sacrifices,' answered Ewedara.

'Sacrifices?'

'Yes, sacrifices to appease the gods. He believes it might be an attack of evil spirits. Sangowanwa, as you know, is a famous medium, reputable in dealing with demonic oppression. I am an herbalist not a seer, hence anything that has to do with spirituality, I hand over to him. He, however, has only come across a case like this once in his entire career. The woman was a young mother who had five children and she had suddenly developed high fever. By the third day, the fever had gone from bad to worse and she became very weak. According to Sango, this lady was brought to him on the fifth day, by which time she had begun to complain of bad echoes in her ears.'

'So what happened to her?' asked Aduni, brusquely.

'Well,' continued Ewedara, determined not to allow Aduni to cut him short. 'Sangowanwa advised her husband to make some sacrifices to appease the gods. Unfortunately, the man delayed in getting the things needed for the sacrifice and the woman died on the tenth day.'

Aduni sighed. Her eyes were bloodshot from lack of sleep and weariness. 'What do you suggest I do?'

'I think you need to go and see Sangowanwa yourself. He'll tell you the things you need to buy for the sacrifice.'

'Many thanks for all your help,' said Aduni to the old man.

'You must not give up on her,' said Ewedara as he got up to leave. 'Be determined to do all you can to fight. Talk to your daughter and pray that she also has the courage to fight. Remember that the body fights disease and death with all its might. It only gives up when the spirit is defeated.'

Aduni nodded in appreciation. Those words meant the world to her and they were going to be the anchor for her boat in the difficult journey that lay ahead.

Aduni lay on her bed that night, weeping bitterly. After a while she began to wail and her entire body shook with grief. She was a woman in pain. The type of pain that nothing could soothe; pain that cuts deep into the soul. She opened her mouth but no words came out; only groans and moans.

Chapter 3

GONE DEAF?

IT was time for another women's meeting in the village of Aje. Ma Moji and Yemi, whose turn it was to prepare the meeting hall, were there early and had started sweeping.

It was an extremely hot day, the period just before the rainy season. Everywhere was dusty. The meeting hall was an old building, the wall was built with red clay, and it was not plastered. The roof was made of dry palm fronds, which was replaced from time to time, especially when the old ones got blown off by strong wind. The hall was sparsely decorated, only a few benches set out on an uneven concrete floor. Two large wooden windows, one on each side of the square building, gave the place natural light.

Before they began to sweep, the two women had to sprinkle water all over the floor, so that they did not choke on the dust.

'Did you hear the news about Kike?' asked Ma Moji, wiping sweat from her brow.

'What news?'

'You never hear anything,' Ma Moji retorted, 'where do you keep your ears?'

'I keep them where they are meant to be,' said Yemi, not enjoying Ma Moji's cynical comments.

'Well I heard that Kike has gone totally deaf!'

'What? Are you sure of what you're saying?' Yemi straightened up and looked at Ma Moji suspiciously, trying to determine if it was one of her false, ugly rumours. Ma Moji, a mother of three, was known for her appetite for gossip. People in the village had a saying that 'if you want to hear the latest scandals about anyone, from street sweeper to village chief, take a trip to Ma Moji's.'

'May the gods strike me dead if what I am saying is untrue,' Ma Moji swore. Then she dropped her broom and raised her right hand towards the roof. This convinced Yemi, because no one affirmed like that over lies.

'Poor Aduni, what is she going to do, how will she cope with a deaf child?' Yemi sympathised.

'You say poor Aduni, how about Kike herself? What an ordeal for a pretty girl like that, to live her life in a silent world. How frightening it must be for her.

Yemi didn't know what else to say, so she resumed her sweeping and eventually did most of it, because Ma Moji, who was only five feet two inches tall, had an unusual penchant for jabbering. She kept on talking in her high-pitched voice, lumbering around the hall, most of the time. Even though Yemi disliked the woman, she was always amused by the way she gesticulated and jumped from place to place when she was talking. Yemi thought Ma Moji was beautiful in her own way, with her thin frame and petite stature.

After they had finished tidying up the hall, both of them sat down to await the rest of the participants. Women played an important role in the politics of Owu. This powerful kingdom owed its success to their wisdom, because, while the men went out to do physical combat with the enemies, they planned strategies for keeping their villages safe. Some of them also worked as spies, and they were always successful in that they mingled well wherever they went, because not many people expected women to be spies.

Yemi got up again and began to look around, trying to find something else to while away the time. I certainly don't fancy sitting here alone with this woman, Yemi thought.

Just then, as if reading her mind, Ma Moji called, 'Why don't you sit down and relax? You keep walking around like a restless chicken whose chick has just been carted away by a kite.'

Yemi ignored her. She went towards the front of the hall to pick up the clay pot where people drank from. She opened it, and gently carried it outside to clean it with the little water left in it. Then she brought it back in and said, 'Please excuse me while I go and fetch some drinking water for the meeting.' Before Ma Moji could say anything, Yemi hurriedly went out of the room. She arrived later with a pot of cool, fresh water; balanced carefully on her head, just as the other women began to arrive. She placed the water pot carefully at the back of the hall and placed a clean calabash on the lid, for anyone who wanted to quench their thirst.

'Where have you been?' asked Ma Moji as she sat down next to Yemi.

'I told you I was going to the brook for some fresh water.'

'Oh, sorry, now I remember.' Ma Moji eyed Yemi disapprovingly. I must be at least twelve years older than this woman, she thought. See how she snapped at me. I wonder what her problem is. She is never at ease with anyone and if she's not frowning, she's pouting, like someone who's carrying the burden of the entire world on her shoulders.

Yemi, a sensitive woman, could not help noticing Ma Moji's censorious look. At least she knows I'm not in the mood for idle talk. That'll get her off my back and keep her quiet for some time, she thought, happy that Ma Moji had finally got the message to back off.

'I think we should visit Aduni at the end of today's meeting,' Ma Moji whispered as the women's leader gave her opening speech.

'That would be a good idea,' Yemi agreed, nonchalantly.

The meeting seemed to drag on and on. Yemi was no longer concentrating. She sat with her elbow on her thigh and rested her chin on her right palm. She continued to stare at the concrete floor as if in a reverie. She could only think of Aduni and Kike. My poor friend, she mused. What an evil world. Is it not enough not to be able to have many children? Now the only one she's got has gone deaf.

Yemi was known by her family and friends as a sympathetic and kind woman, even though she had her own struggles. At the age of seventeen her father gave her in marriage to Yomi, a man who already had six wives. Yomi loved her dearly, and he was protective of the beautiful innocent girl, whose round face and dreamy eyes made his heart skip a beat every time he looked at her. Her youthful smooth fair skin was his delight, because all his other wives were much older. He did not hide the fact that she was his favourite, and this made the other wives envious of her.

Many times she felt so alone in her unhappy marriage and the only friend she trusted and who helped and supported her over the years was Aduni.

Yemi was juggled back to reality by Ma Moji's sharp nudge. The meeting had come to an end. She yawned loudly, turned to Ma Moji and said, 'Look here, I'm off to Aduni's, so I don't think I'm in the mood to exchange pleasantries with anyone. Did you say you were coming?'

'Must you go now?' asked Ma Moji. 'Aren't you going to chat with people?'

'I think I'll leave you to do the chatting,' replied Yemi. 'I'll see you later.' She then crept out through the back door so that no one would see her leave.

Aduni's house was not too far from the meeting hall, only about 20 minutes walk. Yemi met Aduni sweeping her front yard. 'Hello, Aduni,' she called in greeting.

As soon as her friend heard her voice, she threw her broom to one side, ran towards her and gave her a warm hug.

'How are you?' Yemi asked affectionately.

'Very well, thank you. Please come and sit in the veranda away from the scourging sun, and I'll bring you something to drink.' She disappeared indoors, to fetch cold water from her clay pot. She gave some to her friend and she too sat down.

When her friend had finished her drink, Aduni asked, 'Are you comfortable on that seat or would you rather we go to the front room?'

'I'm fine here for now, I always enjoy the view out here, it's so peaceful and quiet.'

Aduni's house was on the outskirts of the village, backing the Homu Woods, where many farmers had their farm land. Aje was a small village of about 550 people. It was situated in a beautiful valley and the land was nourished by the Omitoro water falls. People from neighbouring towns and villages referred to Aje as evergreen, because they never had drought. Leaves and plants maintained their lustre, even during the dry season.

Aduni and her family lived in a fairly large house, built on an acre of land. There were a few palm trees on both sides of the sandy front yard, and Jakobu, Aduni's husband had planted low shrubs round their compound to demarcate it from their neighbours.

Indoors, the walls were tastefully decorated with artefacts and colourful batik clothes. Five wooden high-backed chairs served as part of the living-room furniture. A bright green raffia mat was laid on the concrete floor, in the middle of the room, which matched the light green batik cloth, on the wall. Another door led to a large hallway, which in turn led to each of the four rooms.

There were three small huts in the backyard of the house. Two of them were on the left side of the yard, and these were the toilet and bathroom, and the one that was on the right was the kitchen. Aduni and Jakobu planted an orchard on their land and they also kept rabbits and chickens in a shed at the far end of the back yard.

'We didn't see you at the women's meeting today,' Yemi ventured.

'I couldn't make it. How did it go?'

'It went well, I guess.'

'What do you mean you guess? I thought you said you were there,' said Aduni in surprise.

'I was and I wasn't. Even though I was physically present, my mind was miles away from that meeting.'

By now Aduni was looking puzzled. 'Is there anything wrong; are the children okay?'

'Everyone is fine. It's just that someone told me that Kike is very ill and I feel guilty that I haven't come to see you for a long while.'

'Oh never mind, I know you're busy with your work and all that. It's true that Kike is ill. She is, however, getting better. At least she's regaining her strength and is able to move around now. The only problem is that she seems to be going deaf.' Aduni's eyes were becoming misty. 'I've tried everything I know, but her hearing hasn't improved.'

Yemi sat listening to her friend and noticed for the first time how frail she looked. Aduni, a thirty-five-year-old dark-eyed beauty had a perfect figure-eight shape, enhanced by her long neck, which made her look tall and graceful, even though she was only about 5ft.5. Aduni was not particularly thin, yet she was not a big woman either. Her hair was thick and long, but manageable. She always washed it with her mother's recipe of special herbs, mixed with egg yolk. Her mum had also taught her how to use *ose dudu*, an African black soap, mixed with herbs to keep her skin glowing. However, that evening, she looked forlorn, pale and sickly, and looked as if she had lost a lot of weight.

'Are you sure she is actually going deaf?' Yemi asked after a while.

'Yes she is,' Aduni replied. Many times, she says her ears echo a lot, and when people speak to her, the echo makes it difficult to hear properly. At other times, she seems to be fine. However, I notice that since she had that fever that nearly claimed her life, her hearing has deteriorated.'

By now, Yemi could no longer hold back the tears. She sighed heavily and began to cry. 'It's not fair, life is just so unfair. Kike didn't come until five years after you got married. Since then, you've had no other child. Now the only one you have is going deaf. Why?' she questioned, bawling like a bereaved person.

Aduni answered, 'I don't know, dear friend. I've asked the question why so many times I've lost count. I've asked the trees of the forest, I've asked the birds of the air and I've asked the springs of Ikogusi, for perhaps they know what is hidden from us humans. Alas, my friend, no one could give me an answer. No one.'

Yemi then stretched her hand out, held her friend tightly and both of them wept bitterly. The depth of their sorrow no one could fathom.

'What are you going to do now?' Yemi asked, managing to wipe tears from her eyes as she sat back on her chair.

'I honestly don't know. You see, this type of disability is like a curse in this village. No one knows how to communicate with deaf people. They simply live in a world of their own. Do you know that many times I tell myself it's only a bad dream and that I'll soon wake up to find my child happy and healthy as before. I am still not able to accept this situation. The worst bit is the fact that my husband is away at war. I don't know how to cope with this alone. Sometimes I feel a crippling fear that I might go mad, because sorrow is slowly eating my heart out and if it continues like this, I'll die.'

27

'You will not die.' Yemi was trying frantically to hold herself together for the sake of her friend. 'Where's Kike now?'

'She's having her afternoon nap. I noticed she was getting a bit tired so I sent her to bed.'

Both women were silent for a while. Yemi sat with her head bowed and folded her hands across her chest. After a while she sat up and said, 'Have you ever attended any of Mama Berta's weekly meetings?'

'You mean the ones she holds on Wednesday evenings?'

'Those are the ones.'

'No, I haven't, though she has invited me a couple of times. Why are you asking; have you been to one recently?'

'Yes,' confirmed her friend, 'and the one I went to was inspirational and extremely interesting.'

'Really?'

'Well, as you know, Mama Berta runs the storytelling sessions in her house and each week different themes are discussed. For example: bravery, supernatural encounters, healing and so on. Participants then give their own views of what they have learnt from the stories.'

'Amazing,' said Aduni. 'I must attend one of the meetings myself.'

'I'm sure you won't regret it. I have always admired that elder and that was why I accepted her offer, when she called me two years ago to come and work for her.'

'I still remember the day you got that job, Yemi. I was really happy for you, because you had a place to go to take your mind off things, and you were able to earn some money to take care of yourself and your children.'

'Yes, my friend, and my boss' business is doing fine. She now has eight of us on her looms weaving away each day. She has a lot of demand for her clothes because of the unique designs. Her clients come from far-away villages, towns and even big cities. Last week, we had merchants from Benin.'

'Benin!'

'Yes, Benin.'

'How did they hear about Mama Berta's cloth weaving?'

'Word of mouth, sister, word of mouth.'

'Amazing! The only thing is that no one knows where your boss is from originally. I heard she came to Aje about forty years ago, as a young woman. She never told anyone where she came from or why she chose to live in this village.'

'Well, Aduni, each person to their own. All I know is that she is from Ibadan, the big city. People say she had family problems, hence she moved. I am really not interested in what her past situation was. She never talks about it and I've never asked. Mama Berta is a genuine human being and she is very kind. Since I met her, she's treated me and my children well. She buys clothes for Teni and her siblings and she brings fruits and vegetables to our house from time to time.'

Birds were chirping happily in the trees that surrounded Aduni's house. Sunset was a sight to behold, as the sky had turned to a stream of cadmium orange, and the sun could be seen in the midst of it, like a large round ball of flame. Both women sat there, staring at the strange figures their shadows were forming on the brick walls of Aduni's house.

After a long pause, Yemi spoke again. 'Did you hear about what happened to my neighbour last week?'

'Who?'

'Kola's mother.'

'Kola's mother?' Aduni was trying to recollect whom her friend was talking about.

'Yes, Kola's mother, the woman who's been suffering from night fright since her husband died during the Aferi battle six years ago.'

'Now I remember. It's been ages since I saw her.'

'And here's the good news, she is totally healed!'

'How?' Aduni asked.

'My friend, it's a long story,' said Yemi, as she stood up. She readjusted her wrap-round cloth, as if she was getting ready to do some chores round the house. Then she sat down again, pulled her legs back and placed her elbows on her thighs. She then leaned forward in a 'come-hear-my-gossip' style as she began to narrate her neighbour's story to Aduni.

'Last week, Kola's mum went to Mama Berta's story-telling session and the theme of the meeting was "overcoming life's obstacles". She said the atmosphere there was amazingly calm, as their hostess shared a story with them. She also said that was the first time in six years that she'd

29

experienced such peace and tranquillity. When she left the meeting she began to visualise the story she had heard and applied it to her situation, and since then she hasn't had one panic attack.'

'Did she share the story with you?' Aduni asked her friend.

Yemi could tell she craved to hear the answer. 'Yes, she did.'

This response made Aduni's face lighten up. 'Will you please share it with me?'

'I certainly will,' Yemi promised, feeling honoured to be asked to step into Mama Berta's shoes as a storyteller. She cleared her throat and began the story.

The Elephant and the Spider

'In ancient Kogi Kingdom, there lived a spider called Lantakun. She was good at weaving beautiful webs and in the entire kingdom no one was more skilful than her. She hardly went anywhere without people stopping to greet her or acknowledge her presence.

'As time went on, she became very powerful and soon she was sitting with the kings and chiefs of the land to discuss politics. This made her proud and she was always boastful of her skills and position in the kingdom. One day, she was returning from a trip she'd made to a neighbouring village to sell some of her webs. As she drew closer to her village, she saw two rabbits taking a walk on a carrot farm – one was black and white and the other was brown. She soon got closer to where they were and overheard them talking about the elephant.

'"Have you heard that the chief is going to honour the elephant on the next market day?" asked the brown rabbit.

'"About time," said the black and white rabbit. "The elephant is a powerful animal, yet very gentle and kind to us all."

'The brown rabbit nodded in agreement and said, "He is huge compared to that pompous tiny spider that goes about boasting about how influential she is in this kingdom. Many times I wonder who she really thinks she is." Both of them laughed heartily at brown rabbit's comment and went their way.

'Lantakun was furious. "So they want to honour the elephant," she carped. "I've worked so hard over the years serving these ungrateful animals, yet no one has ever thrown a party in my honour. We'll soon see what they think of their ugly sluggish elephant after I've found a way of humiliating him." Then she crawled away angrily.

'Lantakun immediately began to think of how to carry out her plan. She gathered her fellow spiders and told them a cock and bull story that the king wanted them to weave a very strong web, which would stretch across Emele Valley, where all the other animals would be able to see and admire their work on the next market day. The spiders were excited about this, and they set out to work.

'Lantakun, because of her status, was able to get permission from the king to prohibit all animals from going through the valley for a whole month. For many days, the spiders wove and spun. They worked like they had never done before, and any time Lantakun noticed that they were getting tired, she spurred them on with words of encouragement. "Come on, comrades, you are not working hard enough, don't you want your names to be known in history as powerful weavers in this kingdom? Whenever you feel tired, just imagine the glory that is ahead of you. The price to be won could liberate you and your families from poverty."

'They all believed her and they continued to spin for many days and many nights. At last their work was done. Lantakun tested the web and it was very strong. She'd never seen a sturdier piece of work all her life.

'Then, she went to the elephant, and told him that as part of the ceremony for his big day, which was the following day, he was to go through Emele Valley where all the animals would be waiting to cheer him.

'"But I must take my early-morning swim first and the brook is quite a distance from Emele Valley," the elephant moaned.

'The canny spider quickly searched her brain for an answer. "Why don't you swim at Omitoro River, which is close to Emele?" she suggested. "There's a short cut to the palace from there."

'"Thank you, my friend," said the unassuming elephant. "I will surely do as you have suggested."

'Lantakun smiled wryly as she left the elephant's house. "It shall be said that I, Lantakun the spider, trapped the mighty elephant," she mused. She then went to tell the other animals to gather at the valley the next day to rejoice with the elephant. "I can just see their looks of horror when their hero gets trapped inside my web," thought the wicked spider.

'The next morning, she was the first to get to the valley. Before long, the other animals began to arrive. They were all chatting excitedly about the event that they were about to witness. The loud noise stirred the elephant from sleep. He remembered it was his big day, so he got up quickly and made his way out of his house, strolling majestically with head raised high, trumpeting his way towards the valley.

'When the drummers and percussionists saw him coming, they raised the tempo of their instruments. The king's trumpeters were blowing their trumpets, and the seven wise owls began to sing the elephant's praise as he approached the cheering crowd.

'They sang:

'"*Erin maa wole* [Hail, oh elephant]"

'"*Erin lakatabu* [All hail your highness]"

'"*Ajanaku koja mo ri nkan firi* [An elephant is more than a passing shadow]"

'"*Bi a ba r' erin ka pe a r' erin* [His presence cannot be ignored]"

'Lantakun held her breath as the elephant got closer to where the web was. However, the huge animal was so busy taking in all the praise accorded to him by his fellow-animals that he did not see the trap lying ahead of him. He beamed and waved his trunk to his fans as he went right through Lantakun's web, hardly noticing it.

'The crowd cheered again and again. "Ride on, Your Majesty," they chorused, waving at him. The silly spider watched in horror as the elephant went through the network of webs as if nothing was there. This was the work that she and a hundred strong spiders had laboured at tirelessly, day and night for thirty days.

'Alas, no web is strong enough to hold the elephant captive!

'Lantakun shrieked as if in pain, but no one heard, because the other animals were busy rejoicing with their friend. Some of the cobweb that got stuck to the elephant's head went swimming with him in the river and he came out sparkling clean. He then made his way to the palace, where he was conferred with the honour; "Gentle giant of the forest".'

Yemi paused, took a deep breath and announced, 'That is the end of the story. My neighbour said that when Mama Berta finished this story, she quoted a Yoruba proverb that says: *"Itakun to ni k'erin ma wedo, tohun terin, lo nlo,"* which means, "The creeper that stands in the way of the elephant, will take a swim with the elephant." I was told that she concluded the meeting by saying, "No matter what problem you face, if you know who you are as a child of God, you have nothing to fear. Whenever you're faced with overwhelming odds, try to visualise yourself as the elephant and think of your problems as a spider's web."'

'What a great story, thank you for sharing it with me,' said Aduni. 'I believe there will be a way out of the dark storm that is raging against my family at this time.'

'I'm glad you found your own interpretation in that story,' said Yemi. 'I remember how you've stood by me over the years. It's been sixteen years of hell for me in my marriage and you have always been there to support me.' Yemi meant every word. Some of the many tempestuous moments of her marriage were like nightmares.

One such was the day the other wives accused her of stealing. Their husband had put the money collected at the men's meeting in his room and it had disappeared. The other wives immediately began to point accusing fingers at Yemi. Iya, the first wife, even swore she saw her sneaking into their husband's room when everyone was out in the front yard.

'I wondered what she was doing in your room, but since she is your favourite, I didn't want to stir up any quarrel by confronting her,' Iya lied.

Yemi was shocked and embarrassed, but because she was a timid woman, all she could do to defend herself was cry.

'Those are just crocodile tears, search her bedroom!' shouted the second wife. 'If she is innocent, then we'll look for the money elsewhere.'

Iya went and did a slapdash search of Yemi's room and came out almost immediately with the white handkerchief containing the money, which the other wives had carefully planted there. By now a crowd had gathered, including neighbours who had come to see what was happening. All eyes were on Yemi and some were whispering, while others merely shook their heads in disgust. Many of them actually believed Yemi had stolen the money. She could not handle the shame so she ran away from home, leaving her three children behind. This fuelled more ugly rumours, but she came back after about four weeks, when one of the neighbours hinted to her that her children were being maltreated by the other wives.

The incident did not help her already timid personality and since then, she hardly trusted anyone, except her friend Aduni, who supported her as she battled with low self-esteem.

'I know they ganged up against you so that you will leave that house, those jealous beasts. Believe me, Yemi, your husband knows you did not steal that money and I'm sure he also knows they planted it in your bedroom, but his hands are tied, especially with those scheming witches breathing fire and brimstone down his neck every day. They will be the ones to kill him one day,' Aduni had told her friend, and they had had a good laugh.

This incident flashed across Yemi's mind again, as she prepared to leave her friend's house. However, she forced a smile, and said, 'I want you to know that this storm will pass and you'll smile again. You know, last year, when my son had that terrible yellow fever, it felt as if I was thrown into a place of total darkness and confusion, but light came at last and the sun of righteousness arose for my son, with healing in its wings. So shall it be concerning Kike.'

'Amen,' said Aduni.

Yemi got up and bade her friend farewell. 'I must hurry home now but I'll come back and visit you another day.'

'I wish you could stay a bit longer, I could do with some company. I really appreciate your visit, please give my love to the children and bring your daughter Teni to visit Kike sometime.'

'I will,' said Yemi.

As she made her way home, Yemi couldn't stop thinking about Aduni and Kike. 'Thank God Kike is not totally deaf as that foul-mouthed Ma Moji claimed. Her hearing might still improve, who could say?' she muttered.

When her friend had gone, Aduni went back indoors to her daughter's room. It was getting dark and the Owiwi birds had started hooting. Kike was still sleeping peacefully. She lay on her mat curled up in the foetal position. Aduni went to fetch one of her woven fabrics which she had bought from Mama Berta, to keep her warm.

As she came out of her daughter's room, she heard gangan, the talking drum, in the distance. She listened carefully so as to make out what the message was.

Then she exclaimed: 'Oh my! Pa Dele is dead!'

The drumming was by now getting louder and fiercer, and before long other drummers joined in, and this was their message:

Erin Wo!

Agba ko si mo ilu baje

Baale ile ku ile dahoro

Dele ti rewale asa,

Erin Wo!

The elephant has fallen!

An elder is gone, the village is disrupted.

The man of the house is dead, now there is a void.

Dele has gone to the land of the spirits.

The elephant has fallen!

Aduni ran outside and saw her neighbour, Tito, also coming out of her house. 'Did you hear what I heard?' Aduni asked.

'Yes, how sad. Pa Dele was an honourable and well-respected elder in this village, and he will be greatly missed. I'll visit his widow tomorrow to see what needs to be done concerning his burial. How are you and Kike anyway?' Tito enquired.

'We are taking each day at a time, thank you for asking. How are your children?' Aduni also asked politely.

'Fine, thank you. Listen, if you need any of my children to run errands for you, please don't hesitate to ask. Remember, we are here for one another.'

'I am most grateful, Tito. Goodnight, and may we see the dawn of a new day,' Aduni prayed.

'Sleep well,' said Tito.

Aduni hurried back indoors. She was troubled. The common belief in the village was that when people died, their spirit still hovered around a bit and they could pay a visit to anyone they wanted, before they finally departed to the land of the dead.

'It is times like this that I miss having my husband around,' she said. 'I can just imagine what he would say, if he saw I was afraid. He would put his arms round me to allay my fears and make me feel secure.'

She decided to tidy her daughter's room, so as to take her mind off negative thoughts. Just then, she caught sight of Kike's djembe drum sitting in a corner. Aduni stood for what seemed like forever, staring at the drum, and this brought back painful memories. She sat down wearily on the floor and turned to look at Kike, who was sleeping peacefully on a mat. In spite of many months of illness, she was still a paragon of beauty. People said Kike was every inch like her, perfect teeth, full lips and beautiful large eyes. She, however, had her father's long legs, which made her look taller than her age.

What a waste, Aduni thought. All her hopes and dreams for her daughter seemed to take wing at that moment. She felt completely powerless, not knowing what to do to help her child fight the illness that plagued her.

She heaved a deep sigh of sorrow as she began to relive how Kike's illness had started. She was still playing back all the events in her mind when Kike began to sneeze. Aduni immediately went into her bedroom to fetch *Otutu bila*, an ointment used for combating cold. She then rubbed Kike's chest several times and told her to go back to sleep. She too retired to bed for the night. They were having a special guest the next day. Her sister, Bolaji, would be visiting from Ijohun. She visited once a year and she set out on the 1st of April, and arrived on the 4th. Bolaji usually had to trek most part of the way, hence she spent a few nights in neighbouring villages.

'Tomorrow is the fourth day of this month. I just can't wait to see my sister,' Aduni said, smiling, and she drifted off to sleep.

She was soon roused from sleep by a loud rap on the door. She had only been asleep for an hour. Who could that be at this time of the night? she wondered. She crept out of bed and walked slowly to the front room. Before opening the door, Aduni shouted, 'Who is that?'

'Its Bolaji, your sister, please open the door.'

Aduni flung the door open and exclaimed, '*Kaabo*, you are most welcome.'

Bolaji gave her sister a warm hug and both of them went indoors.

'Where is Kike, my baby?' Bolaji asked.

'Oh, she is fast asleep.'

'I know you were not expecting me tonight, but I was so eager to see you and Kike that I decided to continue my journey, even though it was getting dark by the time I got to Otito village. I could have spent the night there but I decided I must get here tonight.'

'Incidentally, I was thinking about you before I drifted off to sleep,' said Aduni. 'It's so good to see you and I am happy you came tonight.'

Aduni went to the kitchen to cook pap, a type of corn cereal, which was a light meal, as it was already late. Both women then chatted through the night, acquainting each other with events of the past year.

Bolaji could not help noticing Aduni's swollen face. 'My sister, you look exhausted, plus your face looks like it's been kicked by a bull in an arena. Have you been crying?'

'Not really,' Aduni lied, trying not to spoil her sister's first night at her house with tales of woe. Bolaji was silent but she kept looking at her sister, as if to say, 'I am all ears when you are ready to talk.'

'All right,' said Aduni, she did not see the point in pretending. 'I have been crying and it is about Kike.' Aduni went on to tell her sister the harrowing experience she and her daughter had been through in the last few months. Bolaji was shocked. She could not hold back her tears because Kike held a special place in her heart. She then began to ask questions about the cause of the illness, when it started and what could be done to help Kike.

The sisters talked till dawn. Then they decided to catch a few minutes of sleep before Kike woke up.

Chapter 4

KULUMBU YEYE

ADUNI was still sleeping when her daughter woke up. Kike's headache had subsided, though she still felt weak. She went to her mother's room, gave her a quick shove and asked, 'Has my aunty arrived yet?'

'Good morning, young woman, aren't we forgetting our manners?' Aduni gently reminded her daughter that she hadn't greeted her.

'I am sorry, Mother, good morning.'

'That's better. How are you feeling today?'

'Much better, thank you.'

After a short pause, Kike repeated her question. 'Did my aunty come last night?'

'Yes, she is here, she arrived late, after you'd gone to bed. I think she may be out in the back yard, hanging out clothes on the line.'

Kike managed a feeble 'hurray' and went out to the back yard. Immediately she caught sight of her aunt, she hurried towards her. 'Aunty, I am glad you are here.'

Bolaji ran towards her niece, hugged her and held her to her bosom for a long while. She was still overwhelmed with emotion, on account of what Aduni had narrated to her the previous night. However, she didn't want Kike to see her crying. 'Come indoors and I'll show you what I brought for you,' said Bolaji in a shaky voice. They both went indoors and Bolaji gave her niece two beautiful beaded necklaces. One was brown and the other was green.

'You make me jealous and you are going to spoil this niece of yours,' Aduni joked.

'Well, she is a very special niece,' Bolaji answered. Then she turned to Kike and said, 'Come, my baby, let's see what they look like on you.'

'Thank you very much, Aunty!' said her niece joyfully. 'They are splendid.' She tried both on and decided to wear the green one all day, as it matched her yellow batik blouse that she wore with a green wrap-round skirt.

Later that day, Aduni cooked delicious amala, a traditional Yoruba food, made from powdered yam. They ate it with okra soup and fish stew.

'Thank you for the meal,' said Bolaji.

'Let's give God the praise, my sister. Why don't you two go and sit outside under the palm trees while I clear up and I will join you later to hear more news about home.'

'Oh no,' her guest protested. 'You did the cooking, I'll do the cleaning and we can all go outside later.'

Kike was not allowed to do any washing-up that night because of her fever. However, she stood by the door of the kitchen, watching the two women chatting away happily. She didn't want to interrupt their conversation, but at the same time she was reluctant to go and sit alone. She watched her aunt admiringly as she moved gracefully around the kitchen.

'My aunt is so pretty,' she whispered. Bolaji, an exceptionally elegant woman of about 5ft.9, was taller than her sister. She was plump and had beautiful feminine curves. Both sisters had beautifully defined eyebrows, and their large bright eyes always sparkled with delight. However, the glow seemed to have vanished from Aduni's eyes. Some days, you could see dark circles and puffs around her eyes, which told of unbearable sorrow and many sleepless nights.

Nimble-fingered and talented, Bolaji was an accomplished storyteller and drummer, who travelled far and near to entertain people across Ijohun her home town, and beyond. She was an inspiration to Kike who desired to become a storyteller. She was also a skilled sculptor, and her niece was extremely proud of her. In fact, every member of Aduni's extended family sang Bolaji's praise, more so because of her wealth, which she shared willingly with any one in need.

Kike had so much she wanted to tell her aunt, she could hardly wait for her to finish clearing up. 'Aunty, are you going to tell me a story tonight? You are the best storyteller I have ever listened to.'

Bolaji acknowledged her niece's praise with a smile. 'Thank you, Kike. I will definitely tell you a story.'

About an hour later, they all settled down to relax under the shade of one of the palm trees in the front yard.

'Aduni, can we borrow Jakobu's djembe drum for our storytelling tonight?' asked Bolaji. 'It is much bigger than Kike's and it will give us a better resonance.'

'Certainly, I'll go and fetch it,' said Aduni. She went into her bedroom and pulled out her husband's drum from its protective bag and carried it carefully across the passage to her sister.

Bolaji cleared her throat and said, 'Tonight's story is about a village that was saved by a lullaby and the title of the story is "Kulumbu Yeye." Before I start, I want to teach you the song that accompanies this story, so that we can sing it together as I progress.' She then began to sing the following song:

Kulumbu yeye Oyeye kulumbu
Kulumbu yeye Oyeye kulumbu
A o fotun gbomo jo
Kulumbu yeye Oyeye kulumbu
A o fosi gbomo pon
Kulumbu yeye, Oyeye kulumbu.

Bouncy baby, bouncy baby,
I will place you on my right arm and dance with you,
Bouncy baby, bouncy baby,
I will place you on my left arm and dance with you.

*** Track 1 in the enclosed Kulumbu Yeye CD**

44

Kulumbu Yeye Story

'A long time ago, in the outskirts of Jago village, there lived a lioness and her cub, whose name was Kako. The lioness was very fond of her baby and every night before he went to sleep, she sang the song "Kulumbu Yeye" to him.'

At this point, they all sang the song again while Bolaji played beautifully on the drum to the admiration of her niece. Then she resumed her story:

'As the days went by, they grew so fond of each other that they were literally inseparable, until one fateful day.

'The lioness prepared as usual to go hunting for food. Her cub wanted to go with her and said, "Mother, can I come with you? It is boring just lazing around in the sun."

'"No," said the lioness emphatically. "As you know, it is getting increasingly difficult to get good meat near home. Today I want to explore new territories and I will only take you once I know it is safe."

'"All right, I'll wait for you here," said Kako sadly as he watched his mother disappear into the deep jungle. He waited for his mother all day, and he began to get worried when by night time she had not turned up.

'"Please God, keep my mother safe," he prayed, but before he could finish his sentence, he heard a loud BOOM! 'The sound pierced the deep jungle with a spine-chilling echo. "I don't like that noise," Kako said jumping up in fright. His mother was still out there in the forest. He broke out in a cold sweat and began to shiver uncontrollably. "What if....what if...that noise was a gunshot? Oh my, what if mother had been...?" He stopped and swallowed hard. He could not bear to think about it. He then made a mad dash for the jungle and as he approached the forest, he began to shout for his mother.

'"Mama! Mama!" he roared. "Mama, where are you?"

'Soon he heard footsteps behind him and he turned round sharply, wondering who it was.

'It was his uncle Kiniun. "What are you doing out here on your own, Kako? These forests are dangerous for a young lion like you," the lion reprimanded. Then he added cheekily, "this is not a playground, you know."

45

'Kako didn't like his comments but he needed to find his mum, so he brushed his anger aside and said, "I am looking for my mother. She's been out hunting all day and she is usually back by now."

'Kiniun tried to reassure him. "I'm sure your mother will be okay, maybe she missed her way in the dense forest. Now run along to your den and I'll go and look for her."

'"No! I am coming with you!" shouted Kako.

'Something in the cub's voice made Kiniun realise it was pointless arguing with him. "Alright, but make sure you stay close to me as we move along the jungle."

'Both animals continued to search for the lioness and before long they saw a figure under a big iroko tree. They both made a dash for the tree to find the body of the lioness lying lifeless in a pool of blood.

'"Mother!" Kako shrieked as if attacked by an intense spasm. He stood back, mouth wide open, looking at his mother's dead body. Kiniun moved towards him as if to restrain him from harming himself because he wasn't sure what the cub would do next. Kako ran past him to where his mother lay and began pulling her up.

'"Mother, get up and let's go home – its dark."

'"Kako, your mother is dead," said Kiniun as gently as he could manage, for he was also grief-stricken. "Please come with me. I will arrange for her to be taken away from here later."

'"I am not going to be separated from her. Sorry, but I am not leaving," Kako said emphatically. Then he began to sing gently. The song he sang was "Kulumbu Yeye".'

Bolaji started the song expecting Kike and Aduni to join in, but both of them could hardly speak, because they were already crying. Both mother and daughter were wiping tears from their eyes and Kike had curled up to her mum.

Bolaji asked worriedly, 'What is the matter – is the story too emotional for you? Would you rather I stopped?'

'No, please, we would like to know what became of Kako. I don't think I can manage to sing that song though,' confessed Aduni.

'Me neither,' said Kike. 'Please let's continue without the song for now.'

'Okay,' said Bolaji and she resumed her storytelling. 'Kiniun was eventually able to persuade Kako to go back to his den. Before long, all the animals heard what happened to the lioness and they gave her a befitting burial. Mr Owl then called an emergency meeting to decide how they could all rally round to help Kako. Orioye, Kako's aunt, volunteered to raise him as her own cub, but since she was getting too old for active hunting, Kako's uncle promised to hunt for them until Kako was old enough to hunt.

'The picture of his mother's tragic death was deeply imprinted on Kako's mind. Although, all the animals were kind to him and they took good care of him so that he lacked nothing, no one could take the place of his beloved mother. He longed for her day and night and when he realised that he would never see her again, he began to get angry and extremely bitter. He promised that he would one day take revenge on the humans who had killed her. He planned to carry out his revenge when he became a mature lion.

'Many years rolled by and Kako grew to be a handsome, strong and fearless lion. One dark moonless night, he crept out of his den and made his way towards the forest border. He knew this could be a dangerous mission, as he too could get shot by a hunter, however he felt his mission was much more important than his safety. He had waited for the day when he would avenge his mother's death and he was not going to change his mind. He climbed over a steep hill and crossed two shallow streams before he eventually caught sight of Lantoro village, sprawled out in the distance under the great Olumo Rock. Kako made his way swiftly to the village, and as he got nearer, he stopped running. He began to walk as quietly as he could so as not to rouse the villagers.

'"I will give one or two houses an unpleasant surprise," he thought, smacking his lips viciously. "It is pay day for those wicked humans who left me motherless," he said as he hurried in the direction of the huts that lay ahead of him. He saw a flicker of light in one of the shacks. This was where he decided to make his first unwanted appearance to its inhabitants.'

At this point Bolaji asked Aduni for a drink of water. When her mother went indoors for it, Kike, who had been taking in every word of the story with great pleasure, also stood up to stretch her legs. It was a beautiful night, the moon shone brightly in the sky, and the wind rustled the leaves gently. Kike watched as her aunt, scratched her legs. Suddenly, Bolaji

47

slapped her right leg very hard, in an attempt to kill one of the mosquitoes. 'These dreadful insects are having a field day sucking my blood,' she said jokingly, and Kike could not help laughing.

Aduni reappeared with a calabash of cold water and gave it to her sister. She had fetched it from her beautiful clay pot, which was a wedding present from her mother. One of her friends said the pot was from Egypt, and it was one of the many artefacts exported from the ancient land.

'Ah! That was very refreshing, thank you,' said Bolaji 'Do you think we should call it a day and continue with the story tomorrow?'

'No, please, not now,' Kike pleaded. 'I wouldn't be able to sleep, because I'll continue to wonder what happened next. Besides it wouldn't be fair to stop a story like that. It won't be good storytelling, I presume.'

'You are wrong, my princess,' said her aunt. 'In fact, good storytelling uses a lot of suspense. That keeps the flame alive. However, since I cannot refuse you anything, I'll definitely continue the story.' Bolaji was a professional storyteller, who knew how to bring her audience skilfully into her tales, with her voice pitch and rhythm. When she wasn't drumming, she was pacing back and forth, using her entire body to communicate in ways that helped her to connect with her audience. The entire Sonibare family regarded her as a passionate artist, talented in the art of painting emotional word pictures.

'Now let's see, where was I?' She scratched her head as if trying hard to remember where she had stopped.

'Em…you stopped where the lion made his way to a hut where he saw a flicker of light,' said Kike, trying to help her aunty.

'Good girl, that means you were following my story word for word.' Bolaji continued her story.

'The lion moved closer to the hut very quietly, went round the house to the back yard and lurked behind a tree. "I hope I am well out of sight, because I don't want anything to spoil this for me," he muttered. He then began to observe the hut to see how he would attack. He saw, through the side window, a woman coming out of one of the rooms, with a baby on her back. The baby was about two months old.

49

'This young mother looked worn out, a sign that she'd been kept awake all night. As the woman tried to sit down on a rocking chair, the baby began to scream again. Not knowing what else to do, the young mother began to dance gently, and once in a while she looked over her shoulder to see if the baby had gone to sleep.

'"This is my chance," Kako thought as he gently crept out of his hiding place ready to pounce on this unassuming mother. Just then he heard the sound of a door creaking. A man was coming to the loo, which was outside the hut. Kako quickly made a dash for his hiding place behind the tree. When the man had finished from the loo, he rubbed his eyes and looked towards the tree where Kako was hiding; then he yawned loudly, shook his head and hurried back into the hut, locking the door firmly behind him.

'"I could have sworn I saw a creature that looked like a lion behind those trees," he said to his wife when he came indoors. His tired wife eyed him, shook her head and replied scathingly, "That's what palm wine and sleep does to your vision, or let's just say you actually saw a lion and it has come to pay us a visit. Wait…I can hear it roaring now," she continued to jeer at him.

'"You are tired, go and sleep," her husband retorted. But then he began to think about what he just said to his wife. "If I had actually seen a lion, I wouldn't be lucky enough to talk about it, I presume, I'd have become meat for it already," he muttered.

'Kako decided to make a second attempt to pounce on the woman. He tiptoed towards the back door and raised his left paw to kick the door open, but again something stopped him. This time it was a song!

'The young mother was now singing to her baby.

'Kako froze. "I have heard that song before. It is called 'Kulumbu Yeye'," he whispered. He stood there transfixed as he listened to the woman. He hadn't heard that song since the day his mother was tragically killed. He began to have flashbacks of the good old days when his mother sang the same song to him as a baby and he could picture his mother taking funny dance steps.

'Strangely, as the woman continued to sing, her voice began to fade off and Kako could only hear his late mother's voice. That moved him to tears and he began to cry softly. There and then, he resolved not to go ahead with his mission and he decided to go back into the forest.

'I don't think it is wise to make another child motherless knowing the hurt I grew up with, he reasoned. What if the child also becomes bitter and grows up thinking of revenge like I did? What if he later decides to kill all the lions in the jungle when he grows to be a man? These thoughts raced through his mind as he swiftly made his way back to his den. Besides, revenge is not the way forward. The best thing is to put all this behind me and marry my beautiful fiancée, Lewa, and settle down to raise my own family. I will then teach her the song 'Kulumbu Yeye' and we shall both sing it to our cubs, he concluded with a smile.'

At this point, Bolaji heaved a sigh and said, 'That was how the village of Lantoro was saved by the lullaby "Kulumbu Yeye", and now I have come to the end of my story.'

'A most magnificent narrative,' said Aduni as she and Kike applauded in appreciation.

'Aunty, that was fantastic,' said Kike giving her aunt a big hug. 'You are simply the best.'

'I agree,' said Aduni. 'You've always been and will continue to be one of the best storytellers in this generation. You are truly the offspring of Sonibare,' she teased.

'Thank you,' said their guest, I'm glad you both enjoyed my story. She then turned to her niece and asked, 'are you feeling better, Kike?'

'Yes, Aunty, the headache has stopped, but my ear still echoes and people's voices seem to be coming from a distance.'

Bolaji sighed and stared at her for a long while.

Aduni broke the silence. 'Let's all retire to bed. I feel very sleepy already. Goodnight, everyone, and may God keep us safe in the night.'

'Goodnight,' echoed Kike and Bolaji.

Chapter 5

FRIENDS

IT was exactly four weeks before the village dance competition. The event would be part of the annual harvest festival, a time when farmers displayed, or better still, showed off their crops, and people ate and drank their fill. At the festival, village girls entertained the crowd, and there were various prizes for best performing solo dancers and also group dancers. Kike had never danced at the competition because it was only open to girls aged ten to seventeen. She had always looked forward to the time when she could join in the competition, because it was such a colourful event. Winners were held in high esteem and one of the fringe benefits was that they got to participate in other events throughout the region during that year.

Kike had arranged to meet up with Teni to practise new dance steps in preparation for the big event. That day, she waited impatiently for her mum to come back from the market so she could go to her friend's house. Before long, Aduni came in and Kike rushed to meet her at the door.

'Mother, can I go to Teni's house?' she asked.

Pretending not to hear what her daughter had just said, Aduni quickly turned to Bolaji and said, 'A young girl is forgetting her manners again.'

I wish mother would stop doing this, thought Kike. Anytime she wants to tell me off, she does this annoying beating about the bush thing and sometimes it gets me confused. She is never direct when she wants to tell me off, and I find it so irritating. However, she kept her thoughts to herself and apologised to her mum.

'Sorry, Mother, welcome and how was your day?'

'That's better. Now, where were we – what were you asking permission for?'

'I said I'd like to visit my friend Teni. We need to practise the latest dance because the competition is only a month away.'

'Remember your aunty is travelling back to Ijoun today and it would be nice to see her off to the village border. When she's gone, you can go to your friend's house.'

'Yes, Mother,' Kike answered sadly. Her aunt had been visiting for two weeks and Kike had savoured every minute of her time with her. Bolaji, a good organiser, had planned her time, so that she could take her niece to various places each day. Thankfully, Kike did not have a relapse during this period and she was regaining her strength steadily.

On the third day of her arrival, Bolaji took her niece on a canoe trip to Keti village. Kike had never been in a canoe before, so she held on to her aunt as they boarded, thinking the canoe might capsize due to the number of people on it. Bolaji remained calm and held her close to her side as they took their seats, and before long Kike began to enjoy her trip. She listened to people's conversations and gossip all the way.

They arrived at Keti about midday, just in time to see the start of the special festival that had brought them there. There were dancers of various ages, wearing the most colourful fabrics Kike had ever seen. Some wore skirts made with straw, and they also tied dried straw to their heads. The most fascinating ones were the stilt dancers. She had never seen anything like that before.

'Aunty, look!' she shouted as one of the men on stilts moved towards them. She was frightened at first, but when the man gave her some groundnuts she felt at ease.

'Don't eat those,' Bolaji reprimanded, taking the nuts from her niece. 'Take heed not to eat things that strangers give you.'

Kike was disappointed, but because there was so much to see she soon forgot about the nuts. They moved away from the crowd to a quiet corner where a wood carver was designing various ornaments.

'How clever!' Kike exclaimed, admiring a large wooden elephant. She went closer and ran her hands down the back of the elephant. Her aunt bought her some beautiful wooden bracelets and earrings before moving on to see other events.

After a while, Bolaji noticed her niece was getting tired so she said,

'Let's make a move, child, it'll soon be dark and we don't want to miss the last canoe going to Aje.'

'Thanks, Aunty; I've had a most wonderful day.'

'The pleasure is mine, sugar cane.' Bolaji sometimes called Kike sugar cane. She said it was because Kike was the sweetest girl on earth, just like there is nothing sweeter than sugar cane.

They arrived at the river bank just as Mutiu the canoe driver was about to start rowing. By the time they got back home it was dark. Aduni had made them a delicious supper of *Dodo* – fried plantain and goat meat stew. They decided to eat outside, under the trees, because it was a hot and humid night and they had a full moon that provided them with natural light.

Kike wished her aunt could stay for another week or two, because she'd had an amazing time, which she hadn't had for a while. The illness had made her bedridden for such a long time, and this had deprived her of spending time with her friends, Teni, Jumoke and Keji. That was why she was looking forward to going to Teni's house that day. She was however; full of sadness because her aunt was about to leave and it would be a whole year before she saw her again.

That day, the hours ticked by very fast and soon it was time for Bolaji to leave. Kike dragged herself from the wooden bench that she'd been sitting on and began to cry.

'You know how much I hate tears when I am leaving you,' said her aunt, putting her arms round her. 'What you need to think about is the lovely time we've had in the last few days. I want you to promise me you will be happy when I leave and that you'll be a good girl for your mother.'

'I promise,' said Kike, trying to stop crying.

'On their way out, Kike asked, 'Aunty, can I come and visit you someday?'

'By all means, my precious,' said Bolaji affectionately. 'You are ten years old already, aren't you?'

'Yes, I am. I'll be eleven next month.'

'Well, by next year, you should be old enough to travel fairly long distances. My village, Ijoun is a long way from here, but if you are coming to visit, your mother would have to break the journey and you can spend a few days on the road, sleeping over in villages en route.'

'Can I really?' Kike was excited.

'Of course, just make sure you take good care of your little feet, as they'll be doing a lot of walking – more than they've done in ten years,' she added jokingly.

'You've given the dreamer something to look forward to,' said Aduni.

They continued their journey in silence, and Kike walked slowly, dragging her feet in the sand as if that would delay her aunt's departure. Soon they got to the village border and Aduni hugged her sister, bidding her farewell. 'Give my love to Mama and the rest of the family when you get home,' she said, wiping away tears.

'I will,' said her sister who was also in tears. Then she moved closer to Kike. She knelt down beside her and held her close to her chest. 'My precious, I am going to miss you, but I want you to do something for me.'

Kike nodded, sobbing as if her heart would break.

'Do you remember that "Kulumbu Yeye" story?'

Kike nodded again.

'I want you to gather a few of your friends together and tell it to them. That story was a gift given to me by my late uncle and I am giving it to you as a gift – pass it on and let people know that revenge is only for the feeble minded. Whenever people try to get even, they never get ahead. Do you promise to do that for me?'

'I promise, Aunty, but I can never tell a story half as good as you.'

'You can, my child,' her aunty assured her. 'A tree does not grow the very day it is planted, and as I always say to you, the journey of many years starts with a small step. You said you want to become a storyteller when you grow up, didn't you?'

Kike nodded again.

'Good, but before you can become a good storyteller, you have to start by telling one.'

Before Kike could say anything, Bolaji got up quickly, took a handkerchief out of her blouse and wiped her eyes. Then she waved her sister and niece goodbye and hurried away.

Aduni and Kike watched her as she turned the last bend at the foot of the hill, before they made their way back to the village.

'Did you say you want to visit your friend?' said Aduni, breaking the silence.

'Yes, Mother, if it is okay with you. I won't stay too long, I promise.' Then she added, 'Mother, I've been thinking, if I win the dance competition, I'll change the way I walk. I'll hold my head high like this and swing my waist just like my friend Jumoke does.' Kike held her head high in a funny way and began to swing her waist like a grown up.

'Why would you want to do that?' asked her mum. 'If you start walking with your nose in the air just because you win a dance competition, what will you do if the chief's son asks for your hand in marriage and you become a member of the royal family?'

'Mother, that was meant to be a joke,' Kike lied. 'I just want to win this competition by all means.'

'Why is it so important to you?' her mother asked tactfully.

'Well, it means I'll become more popular with the girls and…em….' She looked away and smiled.

'And the boys?' said Aduni jokingly.

Kike said nothing.

'Can I wear one of the necklaces Aunt Bolaji gave me?' Kike tried to change the subject.

'Why not? I am sure I can even find you matching earrings.'

'Oh thanks, Mother,' said Kike joyfully.

By now they could see Teni's house in the distance. Teni's mum, Yemi, was Yomi's seventh wife, so Teni lived in a large house with numerous half-sisters and half-brothers. 'Why don't you run along now so that you can practise your dance before it's too dark,' I will go and see Mama Berta. She hasn't been well lately and I promised to see her today.'

'Can I come along too? I can go to Teni's house another time. I love going to see Mama Berta, she tells wonderful stories and she makes me laugh.'

'I don't think that would be a good idea,' Aduni snapped. 'I told you the woman is ill. Would you consider it good manners to expect a sick woman to entertain you with stories?'

'I guess not,' said Kike repentantly, and she wondered why her mother was so irritable. It must be because of her sister's departure she reasoned. Just then, her mother's voice pierced her thoughts.

'Give Teni's mother my love and please do not eat anything that Teni's stepmothers give to you. I don't trust those women, besides; no one ever knows the next evil they have up their sleeves. Remember that all lizards move around on their bellies, but you never know the one that has bellyache.'

Kike began to laugh at her mother's proverb about lizards having bellyache. I wonder where she gets all these adages, she is never short of them and she seems to have one for every situation, she thought. 'I'll see you back at the house, Mother, and I'll remember to watch out for the lizard with bellyache,' she teased as they parted.

'Please play gently and don't do anything too strenuous - remember you are just regaining your strength,' her mother called after her worriedly.

Teni was with two other girls when Kike arrived at her house. These girls, Jumoke and Keji were her good friends and they had always played together since they were toddlers. The only problem was that Jumoke and Keji never saw eye to eye. They were always at each others throats. Strangely, the two girls were inseparable; wherever you see Jumoke, Keji was sure to be there.

Jumoke, popularly known as 'the village beauty' was nine and a half years old and she was taller than most of her friends, who were older than her. She had snow-white teeth, which she enjoyed showing off from time to time. Whenever she smiled, the dimples on her cheeks formed a lazy zero and she loved keeping them on for a while. Her hair was bushy and long, and she always tied it up in a tidy bun.

The second girl, Keji, was ten years old. She was short and plump and she hunched her back and always looked down at her feet when she walked. The way she carried herself made her look like an elephant making its way through the jungle. She ate anything and everything edible. Her nickname was '*Jeun ko ku,*' which meant 'eat till you die.' The other children were usually mean to her, because of her greed. She never shared anything with anyone, especially food.

Kike, however, was popular among her friends, because of her kindness – and she was known as the dreamer, because, even though she was only ten, she had wonderful imaginings about what she wanted to do when she grew up, the sort of person she would like to marry, and so on. Sometimes her ideas sounded ridiculous to her friends, like travelling around the world, at a time when knowledge about other people and places of the world were not known to them.

Aduni was the only one who never doubted her daughter. She knew Kike was capable of achieving anything she set her mind to do. An example of this was when she decided to learn how to play the mbira and djembe drum. She started taking lessons from a local artist, but she met with a lot of opposition, because all the other students were boys. They jeered at her, and called her names, but she wouldn't quit. She found that she was very good at playing the djembe drum, better than the mbira, so she decided to focus on the former. Within four months she had mastered the techniques and within a year she was playing at local festivals.

Soon after Kike arrived, Keji came up to her and asked, 'Do you know the steps to the latest dance?' Her mouth was full of roasted plantain.

'Why do you want to know?' Jumoke cut in rudely, looking at Keji in disdain. 'You are not hoping to enter the competition, are you?'

'Why not – am I not a girl?'

'Yeah, some girl.' Jumoke was determined to be offensive. 'What an entertainment it would be to see you on the dance floor.'

'Stop it, both of you, why can't you two ever get along?' Teni yelled at them.

'She started it,' Keji protested. 'I wonder who she thinks she is - the stinking prat.'

'Is it time for the name-calling game?' Jumoke thundered. 'Well, take this, fat cheeks.' She moved close to Keji and gave her a big shove.

'Wimp! your only weapon is your fist,' Keji shouted.

'While yours is your fat cheeks full of garbage, you moron!'

'Did you hear that!' shouted Keji, her voice shaking with rage. 'Did you hear her calling me a moron?' She then charged headlong towards Jumoke, raging like a wounded bull in an arena, and knocked her down. Jumoke fell backwards with a heavy thud and everyone exploded with laughter. It was then that Kike looked across the fence and saw that a group of boys were watching the fight.

'Oh no,' she said, knowing that her friend would never recover from the shame. One of Jumoke's pastimes was showing off to the village boys and she enjoyed the attention she got from them. Jumoke managed to get up and ran towards Keji with a devilish look on her face. She hit her hard across the face and held her neck as if she was going to kill her.

At this point Teni's dad came rushing out of the house with a whip in his hands. He gave both girls a thorough beating and sent them to their parents' houses.

'Get out of here at once and if you feel like killing yourselves you can go and do it somewhere else,' he bellowed. He then turned to his daughter and said, 'I never want to see Jumoke and Keji round here again. Both girls are troublemakers. Did you hear that?'

'Yes, Father,' said Teni, who was afraid her father was going to punish her too. He then stormed back indoors.

'I am ever so sorry,' said Teni to Kike when all had quietened down.

'Never mind, it's not your fault,' said Kike reassuringly. 'What I don't understand is why you invited the two of them here today, when you know what they're like. We wouldn't have been able to get anything done, because they are always arguing and fighting.'

'I didn't invite them,' said Teni defensively 'they both turned up an hour ago and I told them that I'd asked you to come so we can practise dancing and both of them said they'd like to join.' I still don't understand why those too girls always argue and fight. The thing is, both of them are my friends and I can't take sides.

'I know what you mean,' said Kike. Now let's get on with our dance. I promised my mum I won't stay for too long. What did you say the latest dance step is?'

'Ko ko ka.'

'What?' asked Kike, trying to make out what her friend said. Her ears still echoed badly, which was extremely uncomfortable for her.

'Ko ko ka,' Teni repeated, laughing out loud because she suddenly realised how funny it sounded. Teni was unaware of Kike's predicament.

'Ko ko ka?' Kike repeated when she eventually heard. 'What does it mean?'

'Don't you remember the song "Bata re a dun ko ko ka"?'

'Oh yes, I do, it is a beautiful song, one of my favourites,' said Kike gleefully, and she began to sing the song:

Bata re a dun ko ko ka
Bata re a dun ko ko ka
Bi o ba ka we re
Bata re a dun ko ko ka.

You shall wear expensive shoes
If you work hard at school
You shall wear expensive shoes.

The two girls sang for a while before they decided to rest a bit.

Kike enjoyed singing the song ko ko ka, but she always wondered what the phrase, 'work hard at school' meant, so she asked her friend.

Track 3 in the enclosed Kulumbu Yeye CD

62

'Teni'

'Yes Kike'

'What does it mean 'to work hard at school? What is school?'

Teni paused before answering.

'I asked Iya, my father's first wife the same question, when I first learnt the song, and she said that school is a place where children go to learn how to read and write. Iya travels a lot, so she knows what goes on in other villages and towns and she said that in big cities like Ibadan, there are schools where children go to learn how to read.'

'Really?' said Kike.

'Yes, don't you know that was how that woman, Mama Berta, learnt how to read that big book that she tells stories from every week?'

'Teni, are you sure Mama Berta went to school to learn how to read that book? She has never said anything to me about going to school, and she tells me a lot of stories about herself.'

'Well, I am not really sure, Teni confessed, but I know that Iya said that's what people do in schools - learn how to read.'

'Do you think we would have schools in our village some day?' Kike asked.

'I don't know, but I hope so,' Teni replied.

After a while, Kike pulled her friend Teni to her feet and said, 'Come on, teach me the dance. I really want to learn.'

'Watch me,' said Teni and she began to teach her friend how to dance to the song.

Both girls practised the dance for a while, until Kike mastered the steps.

'You are a fast learner and you have ears for rhythms,' Teni said admiringly. 'It took me two weeks to learn that dance, you know.'

'Thanks, I've had a good time. You must come to my house next week so we can rehearse again together. I really have to go now, it's getting late and my mother will be expecting me. Thanks again for asking me round.'

Unfortunately for Kike, she had a relapse just before the dance competition and she could not join the other girls in the event. This saddened her and it made her wonder if she was ever going to live a normal life without the fever coming and going at will.

One morning, about a week after the festival, she woke up with a bad headache and she needed the toilet badly, so she made her way to the back yard where the toilet was. The air outside smelled fresh and Kike stood for a brief moment, savouring the unpolluted early morning breeze. She could hear Tito, their next-door neighbour, calling her children to get out of bed. The woman sounded so far away, and her voice echoed. What is happening to me? Kike wondered. Am I going deaf or what? Fear crept into her mind as she remembered Akim, who lived down by the river.

Akim was born deaf; and he never spoke a word. He babbled a lot, hence people called him stupid. No one could communicate with him, and this made him very frustrated. He was well known in the village for his bad temper and people avoided him like the plague. Whenever he caught someone looking at him, he simply threw stones at the person. This was because of the unpleasant experiences he'd had. People made fun of him, pointing at him as if he was some kind of two-headed beast.

Kike was lost in thought. What did I do to deserve this, what will happen to all my dreams of travelling round the world, telling stories and entertaining people?'

Her eyes were aching so much, she could hardly move them. Whenever she tried to look at an object, they stung as if someone had rubbed hot pepper on them. She went back indoors to find her mum already cleaning the house.

'Kike, you're up,' she smiled cheerily. 'How are you?'

'I feel a lot better,' she lied, trying to sound cheerful so her mum could start her day with less gloom.

'Today I will make you my special pepper soup, with smoked fish. I'll quickly go to the market to get the ingredients as soon as Mama Berta arrives.'

'Hurray! Mama Berta is coming.'

'I knew that would cheer you up,' said her mother, smiling.

'I love that mama and I have never had any boring moments with her. She tells stories in a way that makes me remember every one of them and I've learnt a lot of skills from her, which I will put into practice when I grow up to be a famous storyteller,' Kike said joyfully. However, her joy was short-lived when she remembered she was not only going deaf by the day, but also getting weaker, not even knowing if she would live beyond eleven years.

Her mother noticed her sombre look and she knew what her daughter was thinking. 'What do you think I should give Mama Berta as a thank-you gift for looking after you?' she asked tactfully, trying to distract her from her present thoughts.

Kike's face lit up again. 'I know, buy her some kola nuts. Mama Berta is always chewing kola and the last time you took me to visit her, she told me that the best gift anyone could give her is kola nut.'

'Really?' said Aduni who was looking a bit concerned.

'Yes, mother, you look worried – why?'

'My child, I am concerned about Mama Berta. Remember she was very ill last month and I went to visit her?'

'Yes, I remember, what was the matter with her?'

'I can't really explain it. She complained of tiredness and she said her heartbeat was faster than normal. I also noticed that she was sweating profusely. I'm beginning to wonder if kola nut isn't a contributing factor to her illness. Although she seemed much better when I saw her last Wednesday, I still think she should take it easy on Kola.

'You see, my mother once had similar symptoms when I was a little girl and I could remember that my grandfather told her to stop eating kola nuts immediately. She obeyed, and within a few weeks she was back to normal. I think I might have to talk to Mama Berta about this.'

Their guest arrived just as Kike and her mum finished breakfast. She immediately began to help Aduni tidy up the house.

'Don't you worry about us, Kike and I will be fine,' she assured Aduni.

Kike smiled and nodded in agreement. She was excited that her beloved friend was there with her. She sat quietly on her mat, watching Mama Berta sweeping, washing and doing the odd jobs round the house. She had always admired the elderly woman and their friendship had grown deeper over the months. She hadn't been able to go out to play with her friends for a while due to her recurrent illness, but Mama Berta visited from time to time to look after her when her mum went to work.

Kike thought Mama Berta was chic, in her lilac wrapper and sky-blue blouse. She had a lilac scarf to match her wrapper and her earrings and necklace also matched her apparel. They were light blue beads, with a touch of silver round the edges. Her ankle bracelets were stunning, and

Mama Berta had confided in Kike that she never left her house without them. The bracelets were cowry shells, which had been dyed in bright colours. This was Mama Berta's invention although many village girls now wore them. Mama Berta was an average sized woman, not particularly thin but not plump either. The 66 year old woman carried herself well, never sloppy or hunched. Her skin glowed like polished mahogany wood, and her beautiful hair always looked tidy. She didn't have tight, kinky African curls because she was of a mixed race. Her father was Nigerian while her mother was Ethiopian.

Kike began to think of what to say to her beautiful friend.

'Mama Berta,' she called.

'Yes, Kike, is there anything you want?'

'I was just wondering, is it true that your mother was the daughter of an Egyptian pharaoh?'

Mama Berta held her head back, stood arms akimbo and cackled heartily. Her voice rang loud and clear, like that of the owiwi bird, singing its early-morning worship song to its creator. She continued to guffaw the more, holding her waist as if to hold it in place lest it gave way under the strain of laughter. After a while, she stopped laughing and said, 'Where do people get all these stories? The other day, a woman told me that she heard I am a direct descendant of Oduduwa, whom Yoruba people regard as deity. So you see I must be a goddess of some sort. The woman went on to say that it was rumoured in the village that this is why my skin glows. Have you ever heard of anything more absurd?' she asked.

It was Kike's turn to laugh. 'I should count myself lucky to have a goddess as my friend,' she teased.

Mama Berta began to laugh again. 'Listen, child, my father was a cloth merchant who travelled to Ethiopia to trade. There he fell in love with a beautiful maiden and asked for her hand in marriage. The young girl gave her consent and within a few months they were married. She later travelled back with her husband to his native land, Ibadan, Nigeria. This beautiful maiden was my mother and they gave birth to seven children, the first of whom is the woman standing before you today.' Mama Berta dramatically pointed to herself as she said this. Then she continued her story:

'I met Lana my husband, whom I loved dearly, at the age of 19, and we got married when I was 20. Unfortunately, we had no children. Lana left me to marry another woman and after a year they had a son. The shame and grief was too much for me to bear, as people would stare at me and pass cruel comments about me being a barren woman. This made me leave my village to come here. I must say I have enjoyed staying in Aje and people here have been so kind to me.'

'You don't seem angry with your husband for what he did,' Kike said.

'At first I was, but I have learnt to let go. We only pass through this earth once. We can either make our journey worthwhile and fulfilling by being of service to our fellow-humans, some of whom suffer greater loss than we do, or we can allow anger and bitterness to poison our hearts and we miss our divine purpose in life.'

Kike did not grasp Mama Berta's words of wisdom. She was a bit puzzled but then she concluded that the lady was kind and lovely anyway, so whatever she said could only be good.

'Would you like to have something to eat?' Mama Berta asked when she had finished her story.

'No thank you. I just want to listen to more stories.'

'Okay, but first let's agree that today we are going to exchange stories. I'll tell you a story, but you must promise that when you are well enough, you too will tell me one.'

'Me, tell *you* a story, you must be joking!'

'No, I am not. I meant what I said. Now do you promise?'

Kike thought long and hard. What story could she, an eleven-year-old, tell Mama Berta? She was not ready to make a fool of herself. However, her desire for stories was much greater than her fear, so she gave in. Besides, I don't have to tell it today – she said when I am well enough and that could be a good while. I'll find an excuse when the time comes, she reckoned.

Kike looked up at Mama Berta. She raised her right hand as if taking an oath and said, 'I promise to tell you a story in exchange, but, like you said, when I am well enough.'

'It's a deal. Now let me think of a story that might interest you.'

They were interrupted by a loud rap on the door.

'Who is that?' Mama Berta called.

'It's Teni and Jumoke, we've come to say hello.'

'Come on in,' said Kike, trying to straighten her rumpled skirt.

Mama Berta gave her a helping hand and asked, 'Where does your mother keep her bedspreads? I need to pile them against the wall to prop you up.'

'Some are in the wooden box behind her bedroom door.'

'All right, I'll be back in a minute.'

Teni was the first one to pop her head through the door. 'How are you, Kike?'

'Not too bad, thank you. Please come in and sit down.'

Both girls sat down beside her on the mat, and Jumoke said, 'Such a shame that you couldn't be part of the competition, you worked so hard at learning the dance steps.'

'It couldn't be helped, I was very ill.' Kike wasn't too keen on having a pity party of any sort, so she quickly refocused the discussion to the competition. 'Now tell me who won.'

'Have a guess,' said Jumoke, smiling and looking rather cheeky.

Kike looked at their faces for clues. 'Was it you, Jumoke?'

Her friends shook their heads in disagreement.

'You, Teni?' she tried again.

'No.'

By now, Kike was getting really impatient. 'Who won then?'

'Keji did!' Teni dropped the bombshell.

'Keji who?'

'Keji our friend,' Teni affirmed.

'Fat Keji?' Kike was trying to make sure they were talking about the same girl.

'Yes.'

'How could she have won?' Kike still could not believe what she was hearing.

'Well, it was like this,' Jumoke, who loved telling tales, began. 'On that day, Keji appeared on stage, wearing a long blue dress and a beautiful necklace with matching earrings that her grandmother had given her for the dance. She had told the organisers that she was performing a solo, because none of the other girls wanted her in their group. As soon as the drummers and choir began to sing for her, she began to hop around the stage like this, thinking she was dancing.'

Jumoke stood up and began to do funny movements, in an attempt to mimic Keji's dance at the festival. Jumoke bent her hands and feet like a frog getting ready to hop. Her face was a sight to behold, as she spread out her upper and lower lips like someone who discovered that the food she'd just eaten was mixed with dog's vomit.

She looked so hilarious that Teni began to roll on the mat, laughing hysterically until tears ran down her cheeks. Kike was holding her head in her hands, begging Jumoke to stop. She had chortled so much and her head was aching badly again.

When they had all calmed down, Kike said, 'I still don't understand how she won the competition, if she had danced like that.'

'She didn't win because she was the best dancer,' explained Teni. 'She won because, according to the judges, they had never seen anyone dance in such a hilarious way. You see, within seconds of her being on stage, the entire audience was rolling in laughter. The drummers cackled so much they abandoned their drums at some point. One of the men playing the sekere threw his instrument down and guffawed until he began to cough and they had to give him water. The man who announced the winner said it was a difficult decision to make, because everyone danced beautifully. However, it was unanimously agreed that Keji would be the dance queen of the year. Some said she did a better job than Kole the local jester.'

'Have you seen her since the dance?' asked Kike.

'Oh yes,' Jumoke remarked. 'She is now the local champion of Aje village and she is enjoying every minute of her new-found fame. I saw her yesterday, with a group of girls. She was boasting loudly about how she had danced so beautifully that the only person the judges could pick was her. She still hasn't got it that it was the way she made a fool of herself and caused people to laugh that won her the crown, not her skills as a dancer.'

It was obvious that Jumoke was jealous of Keji. 'I still don't speak to her, mind,' she continued, 'not since she humiliated me in front of those boys on the day of our fight at Teni's house.'

Kike looked at Teni and winked. She knew Jumoke would never recover from that occurrence, especially since some of the village boys were there that day, hooting and jeering.

'How is your fever?' Teni asked Kike in an attempt to change the subject.

'I feel a bit weak and the headache comes and goes at will. I just wish I am well enough to play outside with you lot again.'

'I am sure you'll soon get better,' Teni reassured her.

'Let's play a game,' suggested Jumoke.

'Good idea, but it must be one that Kike will enjoy,' Teni said considerately.

'Shall we play "riddles and jokes"?'

Everyone agreed.

'I think Kike should lead,' Teni suggested.

Kike agreed and gave the first riddle. 'It is going to Oyo town and it faces Oyo, it is coming from the same Oyo town and still faces Oyo.'

'I know the answer. It is gangan, the talking drum,' said Teni.

Her friends cheered and clapped for her.

Kike continued, 'Who eats with the king and refuses to tidy up the table?'

'I know that one, it's a fly,' said Jumoke.

'Hurray!' It was Jumoke's turn to be cheered.

Just then, Mama Berta, who had left the girls to enjoy their time together, came in. 'I have brought you girls something to nibble.' She placed two bowls on a nearby stool, one had popcorn, and the other had groundnuts.

The girls smacked their lips, ready to eat their snack. Kike was the only one who would not eat.

'Take a handful at least, if you don't eat, your body won't have the strength to fight sickness,' Mama Berta insisted. 'When you finish eating, you girls should go out and play so that Kike can have some rest.'

When they'd finished eating, the girls said thank you to Mama Berta and Kike before leaving.

'Thanks, I've had a lovely time. Please come back again soon,' said Kike who was sad to see her friends leave.

A few minutes later, Aduni arrived from the market, looking really excited. 'Listen to what I heard in the market, the war has ended and the soldiers are coming home.'

'Bravo! Father is coming home!' Kike clapped jubilantly.

Aduni wished she could rejoice like her daughter, but some ugly thoughts were holding her back. The soldiers had been away for eighteen months and although news about the war came from time to time, no one knew how many casualties there were. She was having mixed feelings. What if Jakobu was dead, or critically wounded?

Meanwhile, Kike continued to express joy that she would soon see her father.

'Let's just wait and see,' her mother mumbled as she went to cook supper.

Chapter 6

HOME-COMING

SIX months had gone by since Kike heard that her father was coming home. She had regained her strength and had begun to eat well; her cheeks were filling out again.

One morning, she went to her mum's room and said, 'Mother, when are we going to see the soldiers? You said they were on their way six months ago, surely it won't take another year for them to arrive.'

'Be patient, child, I am sure they'll be here before the next market day.'

'Which is another one and a half weeks,' said Kike, rather disappointed. She had hardly finished her statement when they heard a loud noise, coming from the street. Gong! Gong! Gong! It was the sound of the village herald's bell.

Gong! Gong! Gong! it went again, sending its high-pitched echo throughout the village. Then the voice of the herald was heard, loud and clear:

'Aje! Aje! Behold the return of your brave soldiers! Aje, behold your sons! Aje, behold your men! They have fought Borgu with their strength and might and victory has been won.'

The villagers began to rush out of their huts, many were conversing loudly, while some were dancing and cheering. By now their noise had drowned the herald's cry as they raised their voices in jubilation. It was a happy moment for the inhabitants of this village, who had waited patiently for the return of their beloved ones for many months.

'Kike, the soldiers are here! Your father is home!' Aduni rejoiced. She then raised her voice and began to sing a popular thanksgiving song:

Ose, Ose O
Ose O
Ose baba

Thank you, thank you,
Thank you,
Thank you, Father [i.e. God].

Kike laughed as her mother danced. She looked so funny the way she held the tip of her cloth, moving her body to the rhythm of the song. 'Mother, everyone is outside, they seem to be going in the direction of the village centre. Let's join them.'

'Yes, my child, come.' She held her daughter's hand and they both went outside to join the jubilant villagers.

It was a huge crowd. Aduni pushed her way into the throng excitedly, pulling Kike along.

'Mother, the dust is making me choke,' Kike called to her mum. The main track that ran through the village was well trodden, thus bare of vegetation. It was exceptionally dusty that day because of the number of villagers stirring their stumps to the village square.

**Track 5 in the enclosed Kulumbu Yeye CD*

'I am sorry, my jewel. I shouldn't have brought you to join the crowd,' Aduni said sympathetically. 'Let's go and sit in front of one of the houses by the roadside till they've all gone. Then we'll follow if you feel up to it.' After about 20 minutes, they got up to make their way to the village centre. When they got there, the place was packed and everyone was chatting excitedly. The noise was deafening

'Are they here yet?' Aduni asked an old woman standing nearby.

'I heard they are just entering the village border. They'll soon be here, my child, have patience,' the kind woman told her.

Aduni smiled and thanked her.

'Let's find a place to sit, Kike. You must be tired.' Aduni looked around for a suitable spot.

'Mother, listen, it's the drums. I think they are here!' Kike held her mother's hand and half-pulled her into the crowd.

'No, wait!' her mother shouted. 'There are too many people. Let's wait here.'

The drumming was getting more intense. It was very difficult for Kike to see anything other than people's backs. She tiptoed, but it was of no effect. She was getting frustrated. 'Mother, I want to see the soldiers marching in. I won't see a thing if we stay here.'

'I know, but what can we do?'

'Why don't we go round the people and see if we can squeeze our way in somewhere.'

They went round and round, but it was as if people stood shoulder to shoulder. There was no space for them to pass through to see the arriving soldiers. Just as Kike was about to give up, she noticed that some children had climbed a big odan tree, nearby. They were obviously able to see everything that was going on, because they kept pointing at people, and they were talking and laughing joyfully.

'I am going up that tree,' Kike announced to her mum.

'No you're not!' Aduni exclaimed.

'If I don't, I won't see anything and the soldiers will soon be here. I must see Papa marching in. Please, Mother, I'll be careful.'

Her mother looked up the tree again, worriedly. 'Okay, but be very careful.' She watched as Kike ran to the foot of the tree and began climbing. She held her breath as she watched her manoeuvre her way through the branches, before she finally chose a suitable one to sit on.

At that moment, the sound of 'Kaabo' filled the air. People had begun to sing.

Kaabo [Welcome]
Kaabo [Welcome]
Ologun wa lode [Our warriors have arrived]
Kaabo [Welcome].

Ayan and his band led the song. People were dancing, singing and clapping. Kike was pointing and shouting. 'They are here! I can see them coming.' Her mother could only guess that the soldiers had arrived, because she couldn't hear what her daughter was saying. There was too much noise.

The leader of the soldier raised his horn and began to blow ceaselessly as the soldiers entered the village. At the sound of the horn, the village chief and his emissaries rose up. They raised their right hands with clenched fists as a sign that victory had been won. The crowd went wild with joy. The soldiers filed by, and the villagers waved their white handkerchiefs.

'There is my husband!' a woman shouted.

'Ah, look, I can see mine,' said another.

'Father! Father!' shouted a young man as he jumped and waved.

Ayan and his band continued to bash their drums while sekere players played their shakers proudly, harmonising with the cowbells. A group of professional dancers also showed off their skills by taking rhythmical steps to the sound of the percussion.

The village chief beckoned to the crowd to be quiet. Then he gave a short speech:

'Welcome, sons of Owu. Your land is proud of you. Your village, Aje, is proud of you. You have fought our enemies bravely and you have won. We will forever be grateful to you, for your loyalty and your boldness.

'I will be throwing a feast in your honour this time tomorrow; please come with your families and loved ones and let us rejoice over our enemies. Once again, welcome home.'

When he had finished, the soldiers bowed their heads as a sign of honour to their chief. The villagers applauded and roared as the chief beckoned to the drummers to resume their drumming. Then the soldiers set out to find their families. However, because of the huge crowd, many of them made their way home, knowing their families would follow behind. Aduni ran to the tree where her daughter was. She called out to her to come down so they could go and find Jakobu. Kike was overjoyed. She chatted excitedly all the way.

'Did you see your father?'

'Yes, I saw him; he looked very frail and walked with a slight limp. Many of them were limping.'

Aduni heaved an agitated sigh. The after-effect of war was always a remarkable experience for all the villagers. Some of the soldiers die on the battlefield and families have to arrange for their burials, while others who were lucky enough to be alive had wounds to nurse. She recalled how difficult it was for her neighbour Tito some years back, after the battle of Aferi. Her husband had lost one of his eyes and he suffered many months of excruciating pain. Aduni was however, thankful that Jakobu was safely home.

Before long, Aduni and Kike could see their house in the distance. Aduni's heart was racing wildly now that she was about to see her husband. What would he look like, how would he react to the news that his only daughter was going deaf by the day? All these thoughts were racing through her mind as she hurried home with her daughter. Meanwhile, Jakobu had also spotted them and he hobbled towards them. He was a tall man, about 6ft.4. He was a handsome forty-year-old, with high cheekbones set on an oval face. Aduni thought he looked much older as he rushed towards them. That must be due to harsh conditions of war, she thought. Even his once protruding belly had diminished in size.

Jakobu was waving wildly and shouting, 'Aduni! Kike!'

It was a moment of unspeakable joy for this family who had been separated for so many months. Kike snatched her hand from her mother's and ran towards her father's wide-open arms.

'How you have grown,' said Jakobu, admiringly to his daughter. Then he turned to his wife. 'And you, my woman, you look as radiant as ever.' He gave his wife a big hug.

Then he led his family indoors and they all settled down for a relaxing evening.

In the ensuing weeks, Aduni kept her husband up-to-date with events of the past eighteen months. Jakobu listened with shock to the terrible ordeal that his wife went through on account of Kike's health.

'It must have been a frightening experience,' he said to his wife one day as he patiently listened to the story of how Kike had passed out and how Tito's mum and Mama Berta had been the ones to resuscitate her. Jakobu must have heard the story a dozen times, yet every time Aduni retold it, he felt a cold chill come over him as if he'd just seen a ghost. 'Let's just thank God that the worst storm is past,' he said. 'Our elders say that if weeping tarries for a night, joy cometh in the morning. My prayer is that Kike's hearing will improve so that she can live a fulfilled life.'

Unfortunately, this father's wish never materialised because Kike's hearing went from bad to worse.

One cold December morning, about two years after Jakobu and the other soldiers came back from war, Aduni woke up to find her daughter crying quietly in her room. She came in and asked her what the matter was, but Kike did not seem to hear what she was saying. Aduni held her by the shoulder and shook her vigorously, at the same time repeating her question, but Kike could not respond, she simply went on crying, because she could not hear a word.

Jakobu heard the noise and he made his way to their daughter's room, wanting to know what the commotion was about. 'Why are you raising your voice so loud, Aduni? It's too early for this kind of noise and I am sure the neighbours are still in bed.' He turned to his daughter and asked her what the matter was, but Kike could not make out what he was saying. She continued to stare at both her parents and then began to sob again. She looked very frightened.

'She doesn't seem to hear what we are saying,' said Aduni tearfully.

'I don't believe that!' Jakobu snapped. 'Nobody goes deaf overnight. It is an abomination!' He then raised his voice and shouted at Kike. 'Get up and come here at once.'

Kike didn't flinch. She knew her father was angry for some reason, and she guessed that it must have something to do with her inability to hear him. Jakobu continued to shout. 'Kike, I said come here at once, you couldn't have gone deaf overnight!'

What he didn't know was that two weeks previously, Kike had noticed that she could no longer hear what people were saying to her. She knew that her worst fear was coming to pass that she would soon go completely deaf. However, she still continued to fight with all her might. I'll fight this deafness as I fought that terrible fever and one day it will go away, she thought.

Unfortunately, Aduni and Jakobu were not aware of their daughter's ordeal. Sometimes when they called her and she didn't answer, they thought it was because she could not hear very well. Little did they know how badly her hearing had deteriorated.

That morning, the realisation dawned on them that their precious daughter would never hear again. Aduni fought back tears and tried to calm her daughter, who was becoming so frightened and confused because of the silence that was enveloping her. She looked at her mother with pleading eyes as if to say please help me break this demon that is oppressing me. Aduni could not maintain eye contact with her daughter. It tore her apart, knowing there was nothing she could do to help. When she could bear it no longer she ran out of the room and went to cry her heart out in the front room. Jakobu calmed himself down and stayed with his daughter for the next forty minutes. He held her hands and tried to reassure her that she was not alone.

'Listen to me, child,' he said, 'your deafness is just a physical barrier that is standing in the way of our communication. What I want you to know is that you can hear me with your spirit because your spirit can never go deaf. Whenever I hold your hands like this,' at this point he pressed his hands into hers, 'I want you to listen to me with your spirit, because that is the moment I want to bare my heart out to you.'

Kike smiled as if she heard every word her father was saying to her.

Jakobu smiled back, convinced that he was communicating with his daughter. 'I do not know why you have to suffer so much. However, I want you to know this for certain, if it was possible, I would trade places with you and I would gladly bear all your pains.'

Jakobu had held back tears till this point, but he couldn't carry on. He quickly excused himself, mumbling something about wanting to go to the toilet, because he did not want his daughter to see him crying. He went outside and sat under the mango tree in his back yard, where he wept bitterly.

After what seemed like hours, Aduni went out to the back yard to clean out the kitchen. She found her husband sitting under the mango tree, head bowed. She moved closer to him and knelt down beside him. It was then she realised he'd been crying.

'What have we done wrong, eh?' Jakobu asked, facing his wife. 'We waited five years before Kike came along and since then we've been trying for another child but to no avail. As if that was not enough, our only child is now deaf. I sat down with her, trying to communicate with her, but she couldn't even hear me. Kike cannot hear me; my child can never hear my voice again.' Jakobu continued to sob like a little child and his wife held him tightly to her bosom all the time.

'I was busy fighting with all my might against Borgu,' he continued, 'not knowing that my own house is under attack. For eighteen months, I fought like a madman, not knowing there was fire under my own roof,' he sobbed.

After a while, he freed himself from his wife who was still clinging to him, and raised his voice in anger. 'It is my fault! Kike had always told me she wanted me to stay at home and work as a farmer instead of being a soldier. My poor child wanted to have a father. Maybe she was heartbroken as a result of my absence. I am sure that was the cause of her illness.'

'Stop it!' Aduni shouted. 'Just stop it right now. You are breaking my heart. What could you have done when you were ordered to go to battle? Could you have said no? Do you not know the result of refusing to obey the call to go to war? You would have been executed!'

Jakobu straightened up and looked at his wife, menacingly. Aduni drew back frightened that Jakobu was going to do something terrible. He spat on the floor indignantly and said, 'Woman, can you not hear what I have been saying? I said my child wanted me at home. I could have been a farmer instead of a soldier. How many farmers do you see going to war?' Then he looked towards the house, with his eyes all red, popping out of their sockets like that of a crazy man. 'For eighteen months I longed to come back home to see my baby. To hold her in my arms and promise her I would never leave her to go to war again. Alas, I came back to find that my only child has gone deaf.'

He then stormed into the house, grabbed his wallet from one of the chairs in the living-room and went out through the front door.

Aduni swallowed hard and ran after him. 'Where are you going?' she cried. 'Please come back.' She continued to run after him, but stopped when she noticed Kike had come out of her room. She was standing by the front door, tears running down her cheeks.

'Mother! Mother,' she cried, stretching out her hands towards Aduni. Her mother turned round and ran towards her and both of them held each other for a few minutes.

Then Aduni made a sign to Kike to come indoors.

Later that night, Aduni sat in her daughter's room, worriedly awaiting her husband's return because he hadn't been home all day. Kike had asked her mum to hold her hands until she slept. The silent world she'd been plunged into frightened her greatly and she was only able to sleep because her mum was there gently stroking her hair, at the same time holding her hand. Her mother's presence in her room was reassuring to her.

Aduni began to wonder where Jakobu could be. 'He shouldn't have left the house in that state of mind,' she thought. 'I do hope he hasn't gone off to do something stupid to himself.'

'No,' she muttered, assuring herself. 'Jakobu is not the type that would go and hang himself. Besides, he loves Kike and me far too much to do that. I'm sure he has gone to drink himself silly. Whenever Jakobu was going through a difficult time, he tended to drown his sorrows in palm wine. That was another problem Aduni would have to contend with: drunkenness!

Chapter 7

STRANGE VISITATION

IT was harvest time in the village of Aje and farmers were busy working on their farms. Aduni had just returned from the market and she was cooking dinner. Kike was feeling bored because she'd been at home all day. She hadn't been going out a lot, and her friends also stayed away because they did not know how to communicate with her. She had even stopped going with her mum to the market to sell batiks because of the way people stared at her, as if she had horns growing in the middle of her head. Aduni found this very upsetting, especially when she overheard people gossiping about her daughter.

Kike now spent most of her days at home, except when she went over to Mama Berta's house to visit.

On this particular day, she decided to take a long walk to enjoy some fresh air before dinner time. She came out of her house, just in time to see her friends Jumoke, Keji and Teni passing by. Kike hurried after them.

'Hello,' she yelled, waving and beaming with joy.

'I thought I heard the rumour that she is deaf,' Keji mumbled to the others, at the same time forcing a fake smile and waving back at Kike.

'Of course she is,' Jumoke answered.

'But she's speaking!'

'When are you ever going to be wise, Keji? The girl is deaf, not dumb.'

'I thought if you can't hear yourself speak, then you can't really speak and....'

'Well you thought wrong,' Teni cut in rudely.

Before Keji could reply, Kike had caught up with them.

'How are you all?' she asked.

'Fine,' her friends chorused.

Silence followed. The girls did not know what else to say.

Teni tried to break the silence and said, 'Shall we play hide and seek?'

'Yes,' said the others, although Kike could not make out what Teni said. She, however, fixed her gaze on her to see if she could get a clue.

In the African version of this game, the rule is that before the person doing the seeking opens her eyes, she must warn the other players that she is about to start looking for them. However, the other girls were not sensitive in the way they treated Kike. She couldn't hear the seeker's warning call, so she was still looking for a place to hide by the time Keji, who was the seeker, opened her eyes and caught her. Kike became upset and Keji was also annoyed at her friend's slow move.

'Go away,' she shouted, giving Kike a shove. 'Who wants a deaf girl in this kind of game anyway?'

Kike was now completely confused. She looked around as if asking for help from the other girls, but none of them came to her rescue. Not even Teni, her good friend. Then she ran as fast as she could away from where they were playing. She looked back as she was about to enter her house, and saw their happy faces as they resumed their play. It's as if they are happy to get rid of me, she thought, as she went indoors.

Then she began to cry. She felt sorry for herself. She used to be a popular girl in the village but now she was deaf, lonely and rejected.

Rejection was the bit she couldn't handle. How am I ever going to have any friends, and who would ever want to play with me again? she thought. It was such a painful ordeal watching her friends playing happily outside.

'These are the only friends I've got left. All the other girls in the village don't want to know me,' she mumbled and began to cry again. She did not see her mother coming in from the back yard.

Aduni put her arms round her daughter, and asked why she was crying. Kike tried to explain what had happened, with a lot of difficulty. She kept pointing to the other girls outside and Aduni eventually understood what might have happened. Aduni could see that her daughter was deeply hurt, so she tried to reassure her. She sat with her for a long while. Kike placed her head on her mum's lap and she felt warm and comforted.

It's not too bad after all, she mused. I still have my dear mother to look after me.

Later, when Teni and the other girls had gone, Kike decided to take a walk down to the brook as she originally planned. The smell of roasted yam filled the air as she passed by Tito's house. She took in a deep breath to sniff the pleasant aroma, which was typical of harvest season in Africa. She then took a left turn, a few yards beyond Tito's house, and came to the path that led to the Omitoro brook. It was a quiet path so Kike did not meet many people on the way. Only a few tired farmers were coming back home after a long day in the fields and many of them were too weary to even greet her.

After a while, Kike's legs began to ache, as she had walked a fairly long distance. She soon found a corn field and sat down to rest. A light wind was blowing the ears of corn back and forth and she began to hum one of her favourite tunes. Although she could not hear herself, she felt light-hearted; hence she got up and began to dance. She still remembered the dance that Teni had taught her, about two years back. She danced and sang the song out loud.

Bata re a dun ko ko ka
Bata re a dun ko ko ka
Bi o ba ka we re
Bata re a dun ko ko ka.

You shall wear expensive shoes
If you work hard at school
You shall wear expensive shoes.

**Track 3 in the enclosed Kulumbu Yeye CD*

88

She danced round in circles until she began to feel dizzy then stopped for a while. She found a small space in the corn field where she decided to rest before going back home. She placed her hands behind her head, to shield it from the stony ground, and she watched with fascination the movement of the clouds above.

Her rest was interrupted by a tap on her shoulder. She turned round sharply to see a girl of about her age, saying hello. The girl was looking radiant in her navy blue batik skirt and blouse.

'Hello,' Kike replied.

My name is Seyi, what's yours?' the stranger asked.

'Kike.'

'What a lovely name.'

'Thank you, so is yours.'

At that moment Kike forgot she had any disability. The girl seemed to understand what she was saying anyway, and strangely, Kike felt she could hear what the girl was saying as well.

'Do you mind if I sit here with you?' the girl asked politely. 'I have no one of my age to play with.'

'I don't mind at all, please sit down.'

'That song you were singing is beautiful,' Seyi ventured.

'Thank you. It is one of my favourites, why don't we both sing it?'

'But I don't know the words of the song.'

'Never mind, I'll teach you, it's so easy to learn.'

They got up, and held hands, ready to dance. Kike first taught Seyi how to sing the song, and then they sang it through several times, dancing and clapping as well.

After a while, Seyi said, 'Let's rest awhile.' She then reached for her pocket and brought out a snack.

'What's that?' asked Kike.

'It's called *dodo Ikire*. It's made with very ripe plantain, mashed, seasoned and fried in hot oil.' She offered Kike some and ate the rest. After eating, Seyi said, 'Would you like to come with me to visit a lovely family who live on the other side of the hill?'

'What hill? There aren't any hills in this part of the village; I know this place like the back of my hand.'

'Well, you just have to trust me then,' Seyi said, smiling. 'Come on, let's have a race.'

Kike was a bit reluctant to wander far away from home.

'Come on, it's going to be fun.'

'All right,' said Kike, running to catch up with Seyi. They went through a narrow pathway in the corn field until they came to a hill, which they climbed without much difficulty. As they descended the hill on the other side, Kike beckoned to the other girl to stop. Then she said, 'You seem to know this area very well.'

'Yes, I grew up here.'

'Why haven't I seen you round here?' Kike asked suspiciously.

'Well, my parents wouldn't allow me to go too far from our house. We live down by the big river on the outskirts of Aje village'

'I see,' said Kike, still not convinced she could trust the girl.

They soon came to the bottom of the hill where there was a small cave, the entrance of which was lined with bamboo leaves. 'I'm taking you to visit my friends who helped me a great deal when I was ill a few months ago. They taught me a lot of things, which has helped me to find joy and fun again.'

Kike was hardly listening to Seyi. She stood still, looking suspiciously at the cave they were about to enter.

'Who lives in that cave? I am not going in there. What if it's the home of a fearful animal or a mean giant or some cave spirit?

Seyi began to laugh.

'What's so funny?'

'It was what you just said about dangerous animals and giants. I already told you we are visiting my friends. The man of the house is called Matthew and his wife is Priscilla. They have a guest staying with them whom I'm sure you will find very interesting. Now come, I don't want to say too much. Get to meet them yourself and you'll love them.'

Kike's heart was now beating very fast. She could hear it thumping, like the gathering drum used to call villagers to important meetings. She was frightened. What if this is a trap? How can I even trust this girl? she questioned in her mind.

Then, as if Seyi was reading her mind, she said, 'you are in doubt whether you should trust me or not.'

91

'Oh no,' Kike lied. It's just that....'

'Never mind, I quite understand. After all, you only met me for the first time today. I am sorry to have put you through this. I only thought it'd be nice to take you to my friends who have helped me so much. They...'

Before she could finish, a middle-aged woman came out of the cave. 'Quick, hide, don't let her see us. If she does, she'll insist we come in for dinner, and I can see you are not too keen,' said Seyi.

Kike stared at this woman with mouth wide open. She had never seen anyone of that skin colour before. The woman was not brown like all the people she was used to seeing. She was fair with straight, brown hair, which she tied into a bun. Her nose was quite long and pointed, and her lips were rather thin. She was a beautiful woman, slim and tall, about 5ft.9. Kike stood transfixed, as if she had seen a ghost.

The lady turned round and saw Kike staring at her. She smiled and said hello in a strange accent and Kike let out a loud scream and began to shiver. She remembered the day her grandfather came to visit and he told her a story about the spirits of the cave. He swore by his mother's grave that he had seen one of them himself. His description of these spirits fitted this woman perfectly. Although Aduni had dismissed the story as a myth, Kike still trembled in horror any time she remembered the stories.

'What must I do when I see any of them?' she had asked her grandfather.

'Scream, child,' he warned. 'Scream non-stop, because they hate noise. Don't let them touch you, and if they insist on coming near you, head-butt them directly on their long nose and make sure you break it. That is where their power lies.'

Grandpa's words echoed in Kike's ears and she continued to scream. Then she began to run away. Seyi was shocked and she ran after her.

Priscilla, the woman whose appearance had scared Kike, quickly ran after them, shouting, 'What is the matter? Seyi, who is this girl and why is she so frightened?'

'I don't know why she is frightened. I met her just this afternoon in the corn field on the other side of the hill, and I brought her here to meet you and the rest of your family but I'm surprised at the way she's behaving.'

By now, Priscilla had caught up with them. 'Wait,' she said to Kike, but when she stretched out her hand, Kike let out another loud, ear-bursting yell. This time, the noise was so loud that Priscilla had to block her ears.

'Yes!' said Kike gleefully. 'Grandpa was right – these spirits definitely hate noise.'

She turned to Seyi who was by now too shocked and embarrassed to do anything more. 'Run, Seyi! Run for your dear life!' she cried. 'This is one of the spirits of the cave. My grandfather told me about them and she's the perfect picture of what he described. Come; let's run away.'

'Will you shut up!' shouted Seyi in anger. 'This is my friend Priscilla and her husband and children live in that cave. Don't you know the difference between a real person and the mythical characters your grandfather has been feeding your imagination with?'

Kike did not answer her, she was busy eyeing Priscilla, watching her every move. She was determined that if she came any closer, she would head-butt her and break her nose.

'Calm down, child,' said Priscilla, who by now decided not to go any closer to Kike. It is wise I keep my distance if she is afraid of me, she thought.

She nodded in the direction of Seyi to be quiet and not be angry with Kike.

'I don't think your friend has ever come in contact with someone from a different race,' she told Seyi. 'Please be patient with her.' She then sat down and smiled. 'I'm not coming near you if you don't want me to,' she said with a strange accent. Although she spoke Yoruba, which was Kike's local language, you could tell it was with great effort, and her voice sounded like she spoke through her nose rather than her mouth. 'My name is Priscilla and I'm from England. I've come to this part of the world on missionary work. You see, there are different people living in other parts of the world who are not brown like you are. Our skin colour is different, and so are our features, but we are also humans like you.'

She then reached into her pocket and brought out some figs and dates and began to eat, to Kike's surprise.

'See, we eat fruits and food like you do,' said Priscilla, and she offered the frightened girl some of her fruit. Kike shook her head, but she was beginning to calm down.

'Now tell me your name,' said Priscilla.

Kike was still tongue-tied.

'You don't need to be afraid,' said the lady.

Still, Kike continued to survey her from head to toe, and then she looked at Seyi who was now standing beside Priscilla and holding her hand. If Seyi said this was the friend who helped her when she was ill and she was not terrorised in any way, then, maybe it is I who is being silly, she thought. How about grandfather's story? How could his description of the cave spirits fit this woman so perfectly? Why has she chosen to live in a cave and not in the village? A thousand and one questions raced through her mind.

At last, she decided to honour Seyi by trusting her. After all, she was the only one left for her now as all her friends had deserted her because of her condition.

'Come and meet the rest of the family and have dinner with us,' said Priscilla, breaking the silence.

Kike hesitated before taking calculated steps towards the woman and Seyi. Priscilla then turned round and led the way back to the cave.

'I'm really sorry for the way I behaved,' Kike whispered to Seyi as they neared the entrance of the cave.

'Don't you think the person you ought to apologise to is Priscilla? At least you decided to trust her not to eat you up so it's still a happy ending,' she added cynically.

The cave was pleasantly warm and tastefully decorated. Beautiful pictures and artefacts were hung on the wall. Priscilla ushered them into the main part of the cave, which served as both sitting room and dining-room. There were low wooden chairs placed all around the room and in the centre was a rectangular-shaped wooden table. On it was a round blue jar, filled with Hibiscus and Pride of Barbados flowers, which brought more colour to the lovely place. The floor was uneven, but spotlessly clean. In a far corner was a hollow place that looked like it was hewn out of the rock of the cave.

On the wall just above the hollow place was a massive picture and the man in it caught Kike's attention. She stared at it for a long while, and something about the man's face made him look happy and sad at the same time. Suddenly, it seemed as if the man moved his eyelids and this made Kike jump.

'What is it, my dear?' enquired Priscilla, putting her arm round Kike's waist affectionately. Then she followed Kike's gaze and said, 'Oh, you are looking at the picture of our friend Jesus.'

'Jesus!' Kike repeated. 'What a lovely name. Who is he?'

'We will tell you about him in a minute. Come to the table and have supper with us. Then she led Kike and Seyi to the large wooden table.

A few minutes later, they were joined by the lady's two daughters, Rebecca and Sarah. Later, Matthew, Priscilla's husband came in with their guest, Paul.

When everyone was seated, Priscilla introduced Kike to her family but she never mentioned their dramatic meeting outside the cave. She just said, 'Meet Kike, Seyi's friend. Seyi has brought her here to meet us all.' Everyone then greeted Kike warmly before they began to eat.

Dinner was roast beef with sweet potato and gravy. It was delicious and they washed it down with cool water drawn from a massive clay pot in another part of the cave which served as a kitchen.

After dinner, Matthew, asked Paul to lead the family prayer. Paul got up and took a black leather-bound Bible from the centre table. Then he sat down again and began to leaf through the book.

After a while, he raised his head and said, 'First, I would like to read to you from my ancient book of wisdom. The passage I am reading is Psalm 139, verse 14.

"Praise you because I am fearfully and wonderfully made."'

He also read from the book of Genesis 1:27

So God created man in His own image,
in the image of God He created him,
male and female He created them.

When Paul had finished reading, he began to tell them the creation story as written in Genesis, the first book in the Bible. He began to explain the second passage that he read, saying human beings were the greatest of all creation and they have the power to be fruitful and creative. He continued to preach for the next twenty minutes, after which he paused and asked, 'What have you learnt from what I read to you today?'

Rebecca raised her hands to answer the question. She was 15 years old, while her sister was 13. Kike kept staring at Rebecca and Sarah. Both of them looked very much like their mum, tall and slim with large blue eyes. Both sisters also had blonde shoulder-length hair. Kike thought they inherited their colouring from their father, because their mum's hair was auburn.

Paul acknowledged Rebecca and told her to answer the question.

She cleared her throat dramatically, and said, 'I think we need to know who we really are because it helps us to realise why we are here on earth, or better still, what we are created to do on earth. Life could be meaningless if we don't know our mission in life. My parents know they are meant to work as missionaries, and they are now working on that mission, hence their joy and sense of achievement.'

'Paul thanked Rebecca before he continued with his preaching.

'You see, knowledge of who we are, gives us hope in difficult situations. We can overcome problems, trials and tribulations when we have hope. Hope helps us connect to the supernatural power of God, which is made available to everyone.'

Paul concluded by saying, 'As you go through life, you may encounter a lot of challenges. People may misunderstand you and treat you unfairly. Sometimes, it seems your dreams have taken wings and flown away, leaving you helpless and weary. However, hold on to this knowledge - that you can do all things through Christ that gives you strength.'

Everyone was listening attentively to Paul who spoke with immense authority.

This man is a great orator, thought Kike. His words are so powerful and refreshing that I feel so good about myself already.

Paul ended the meeting by saying the grace, after which everyone applauded and thanked him.

Kike learnt a lot about positive thinking from Paul's simple message, and she yearned and craved for more, but it was getting dark and she felt it was time to leave.

'I must hurry back home now. Thank you very much for inviting me to have dinner with your family,' she said to Priscilla shyly, 'and I am sorry for embarrassing you earlier on.'

Priscilla smiled and gave her a warm hug.

Everyone hugged Kike and told her they were sorry to see her leave.

'I'll see Kike to the door and I'll come back to help you with the washing-up,' said Seyi.

As Kike stepped out of the cave, she felt cold water splashing on her face. Wondering where the water came from, she looked up to the sky, only to see that it had started raining.

The sun had set and she found herself lying on her back in the corn field. She got up quickly to look for the cave and her friend Seyi but nothing was there except rows and rows of corn. Suddenly she realised she had fallen asleep.

Had she been dreaming?

She refused to believe this and instead began to call for Seyi.

'Seyi! Seyi!' she called, but she could not even hear herself speak. Everywhere was silent as it used to be.

An overwhelming sense of loss crept upon Kike, when she realised she'd been dreaming. Where is my friend? Why am I back in this silent world? Where is the cave house, where are all those nice people? She began to cry. 'How sad and how unfair,' she muttered as she got up and hurried home so as not to be drenched by the rain.

By the time she got home, her clothes were soaked and she was dripping all over the floor of the house.

'Where on earth have you been?' Aduni shouted as if her daughter could hear her. Kike could sense from her mother's body language that she was angry. 'Don't just stand there, come and change your clothes before the cold gets to your chest,' she said, pulling her daughter towards her bedroom. She got out an old cloth from her wooden box and gave it to Kike.

'Here, take that and wipe yourself and then change your clothes,' said Aduni.

At bedtime, Kike could not sleep. She was pondering on the dream she had earlier on in the corn field. Paul's words began to come back to her. '...What problems are you facing? Is it sickness, hopeless situation? The joy of the Lord is your strength.' She found herself repeating those positive affirmations as she drifted off to sleep.

'What a strange visitation!' she whispered.

Chapter 8

RAYS OF HOPE

'THERE goes Mama Berta,' said Aduni, waving excitedly to the tall, graceful woman making her way through the crowd. 'Mama Berta! she shouted, trying to raise her voice above the din in the market. The cockerel in her hand was flapping wildly, wanting to be set free.

The elderly woman turned round to see who was calling. When she saw Aduni she waved back and hollered, 'Wait there. I'll cross over to where you are.'

Aduni watched the elegant woman as she manoeuvred her way to where she was. She wore a bright green batik blouse and a white wrap-round skirt and matching jewellery. I wonder how she manages to look so radiant every single day. Her skin glows even in the dark and her hair is always in place, she mused. Soon Mama Berta got to where she was and greeted her warmly.

'Good afternoon,' Aduni responded, curtseying at the same time. 'I hope you are well.'

'Yes I am, thank you, and how is Kike?'

'She is fine. I actually came to the market because of her. You see, yesterday she started her monthly period and you know that according to tradition I am meant to celebrate her transition into womanhood by buying her a cockerel.'

'Congratulations,' rejoiced Mama Berta in her happy singsong voice. 'How does she feel about it?'

'Well, she is still very upset. I haven't been able to explain much to her yet. I don't know how to. Her father and I still find it so difficult to communicate with her. This should have been a day of joy for us all, but it is joy mingled with heavy sorrow,' Aduni lamented.

'Did you prepare her for it?'

'Absolutely not!' Aduni was shocked that Mama Berta could ask such a question. 'That is not the sort of thing you discuss with a child; when it happens it happens.' She paused and gave Mama Berta a questioning look. When she got no response, she continued defensively, 'I wasn't prepared for it and neither was anyone I know.'

'Well then, it is about time young girls are made aware of these things before they happen; don't you agree, Aduni? Can you imagine how much better it would have been if Kike knew she was going to start her menstrual cycle some day?'

Aduni nodded in agreement. 'But I never thought she would go deaf and I...'

'Please don't get me wrong,' said Mama Berta, evidently sensing Aduni's defensive tone. 'I am not trying to make you feel bad, I am speaking generally about the need for us women to change our attitude to all these taboos that we hold sacred, which debar us from educating our children.'

'I do see your point and it makes a lot of sense,' Aduni agreed, and then she quickly changed the subject. 'By the way, how is your weekly art and craft workshop going?'

'Very well, thank you. So far, four girls and three boys have shown interest in some of the workshops. I have held series of meetings with parents in the village, to encourage them to send their children to learn one or two crafts. You never know when these skills might become useful. Look at me, for example. When my husband left me for another woman, I thought I would not be able to survive on my own, but after the initial shock, I was able to fend for myself, by using all the skills I learnt from my parents as a young girl.'

Aduni nodded in agreement and said, 'The reason I asked is that I want Kike to join one of your classes. She is a very intelligent girl and I don't want her to waste away. She is so skilful in playing the djembe drum, and as you know, and she sings beautifully. However, because of her condition, she has stopped all that and I can see frustration building up in her. She no longer laughs; in fact you can hardly get her to smile.'

Aduni paused, frantically fighting to hold back tears. 'For God's sake,' she continued, bursting with rage, 'my child is just getting to her prime but it is as if she is at life's sunset. Her light is gently turning into darkness right before my eyes and I can't even do anything about it.'

Mama Berta took her by the hand and led her to a quiet corner, near a fishmonger's stall. 'Aduni, look at me,' she said, and she held her young friend's face in her hands, gently. 'Let us make a promise to ourselves and this is between you and me. We are not going to allow this problem to drown us. With the help of God, we will do our best for Kike to see that she sails through these turbulent waters. Would you like to agree with me on this?'

Aduni paused before replying, 'I will be truthful to you; I am now getting weak and despondent. I don't even want to fight this never-ending battle any more. In fact, I could just sleep and die so that I do not have to wake up and see another day of my child struggling with this curse that has been placed on her.'

'Those are powerful words, Aduni. You and I have talked about the power of words. This situation seems hopeless and you don't know what to do about it now. However, I believe Kike will live to fulfil her destiny. You see, your daughter is a very strong girl and extremely determined. What we should do is to support her. She will pull through this and come out on the other side victorious. Let's just wait and see.'

Aduni nodded to show that she was taking in what Mama Berta was saying.

'How old is Kike now?'

'She is fourteen years old. Why are you asking?'

'It's just that I started my monthly periods when I was fourteen as well, and I can just picture that day now. Anyway back to what we were discussing. Bring your daughter to see me next week. I am happy to take her through whatever programme she fancies.'

'Thank you very much – you always bring me hope when I need it most. I will never forget your kindness to my family. May God reward you bountifully. I'll bring Kike to your house next week.'

Back home, Kike was coming out of the bathroom when her mother arrived home. 'Mother, you are back,' she said, hastily disappearing into her room. She hadn't recovered from the shock of what happened that morning.

Aduni had woken up very early to go and visit her friend, Yemi, who had just had a baby. Suddenly, she heard her daughter screaming for her.

'Mother! Mother! Come quick,' Kike was shouting as loud as she could, hoping her mum would hear her. Sometimes she wondered if anyone heard when she spoke. Even though she couldn't hear a thing, she still spoke very clearly, but it was difficult for her to know this fact.

It was Jakobu who heard her first and he came running to where she was.

'What is it?' he asked when he got to her room.

'I want Mother,' Kike replied firmly, looking rather disturbed.

Meanwhile, Aduni too had heard her daughter calling and she rushed towards her room. 'What is the matter?' she asked Jakobu as he came out of Kike's room.

'She said it is you she wants,' he said, looking puzzled.

Aduni hurried to where her daughter stood, wide-eyed.

'Mother, look!' she screamed.

Her mother looked towards where she was pointing and cried, 'Oh, my baby, my baby.' Aduni held her daughter and she began to dance around the room.

Kike screamed the more, and shook her mother as if to make her understand what was happening.

'Mother, I am bleeding!' she yelled. 'I am bleeding and YOU are dancing.' She looked a pitiable sight. She had no clue why she was bleeding and she expected her mother to panic and do something to stop it before she bled to death, or so she thought. Hence she was taken aback by her mother's reaction. When Aduni did not stop dancing and crying 'Oh my baby,' Kike concluded that her mother was going crazy.

My worst fear has come to haunt me, she thought. Kike had always feared that her mother might one day lose her mind because of all the problems she was going through on account of her illness. She had started bleeding the previous night but was afraid to tell her mother so as not to add to her sorrows. However, when the bleeding did not stop after about twelve hours, she had no choice but to call for her.

I knew her mind would not take any more sorrows, poor mother, Kike thought as she watched her mum dance around her room. At this point, she began to cry, thinking Aduni had gone completely nuts.

'Oh no, don't cry,' said her mum. She held her again and began to twirl round, singing and clapping.

'Mother, are you all right?' Kike ventured.

Aduni nodded happily and gave her daughter a hug. 'I am all right, my child, it is my moment of joy to see my child become a woman.'

Jakobu, who was by now getting impatient, came into the room. 'Now let's have it, what is this all about?'

'Kike has become a woman. She has just started her menstruation,' Aduni announced ecstatically.

'Oh! em...good. I mean, good girl,' muttered Jakobu, obviously embarrassed. 'I'll wait outside while you sort her out,' he said to his wife as he hurriedly made his way out of the room.

Aduni turned to face her daughter who was waiting patiently for her mother to explain what was happening to her. 'How do I begin to tell you that today you have become a woman, eh, my child? Let's get you tidied up and then I'll see how I can explain things to you.'

She took her daughter to the bathroom and helped her get cleaned up. She then taught Kike how to use sanitary towels, and how to change them regularly.

Kike nodded when she had understood what her mother was saying. Then she went back to her room, still in shock. The worst part of it was that she had no foreknowledge of the situation, no one had ever discussed with her that she was going to start bleeding some day. She also thought she would from then on continue to bleed every single day for the rest of her life. Unfortunately, she thought she was the only one who was experiencing menstruation and that it was an illness or disease just like her deafness.

A few days after this incident, Aduni announced to her husband that she wanted Kike to start attending one of Mama Berta's art and craft workshops.

'How is she going to cope?' Jakobu exclaimed.

'She will. Kike is a brilliant child and I hate to see her sitting down and doing nothing all day. That child is not cut out for idleness and that alone could kill her before her time. Have you noticed how moody she's been lately?'

'I know, but how does a deaf child…?'

'You just have to trust me on this one,' Aduni cut in sharply.

'Okay, I trust you to do what is best for her,' Jakobu said reassuringly.

Aduni wasted no time at all, and the following week she took Kike to see Mama Berta.

Mama Berta's house epitomised her riches and splendour. She had acquired a massive land some thirty years back. The land, which was about five acres in all, was well located with stunning views. It was directly opposite the Omitoro water Falls. This water fall was half a mile from Mama Berta's house and one could just about catch a glimpse of it in the distance.

The sound of water as it gushed down and splashed over the rocks was soothing and refreshing both day and night. Many evenings Mama Berta would ask one of her workers to place her favourite armchair in the veranda, where she could listen to the 'music of the river,' as she called it.

Trees and hedges were planted round the land to demarcate it from neighbouring plots of land. The front yard that led to the veranda of the first building was huge, about a third of an acre. It had a beautiful garden of shrubs, flowers and palm trees, which gave the house the look of a palace. Her gardener, a hard-working young man called Wuyi, looked after the garden well, tending and maintaining it to a high standard, to the delight of his boss. Consequently, when he got married, Mama Berta built him a small hut with three rooms. With the load off his mind of getting suitable accommodation for his young family, he was able to concentrate more on his gardening.

A long pathway led from the gate to a veranda in front of the big house. This was where Mama Berta relaxed in the evenings. There were six wooden chairs, a table and a swing chair, which added to the beauty of the porch.

There were four buildings in Mama Berta's compound. There was the main building, which was the biggest of the four.

Mama Berta lived in this big house with her housekeeper, Sade, an eighteen-year-old girl who had been living with her for five years. She was the first child of her parents, but unfortunately her mother had died when she was giving birth to her sixth child. This tragedy was a huge blow to her family, because they all depended on the mother to cater for them as their father was crippled. He used to work as a palm wine taper, but one day he fell from a palm tree and broke his back.

Although their extended family rallied round to help the children after their mother's death, the void she left could not be filled. The children were sent to different relatives and the family was never together again. Sade was living with one of her aunts, a mean woman, who only took her in because relatives forced her to. The woman was forever beating her up, saying she was lazy and wicked. Mama Berta came to her rescue one day, when she found her lying on the street, after she'd been kicked out by her aunt. She went to see the head of their clan, who after much persuasion agreed that Sade could live with her.

Mama Berta always remembered how hard she fought to convince the old man to let his great-grandchild live with her. 'We would rather have Sade live with a blood relative than with a foreigner,' he had said to her face. A few years later, when Mama Berta's housekeeper left the village, Sade told her hostess not to look for another housekeeper because she would like to start working for her, and Mama Berta agreed.

From the porch in front of the house, a large door led to the sitting-room, which was ostentatiously decorated with artefacts, carvings and paintings. The one that stood out and which Kike loved most was a painting from Ethiopia. Every time she came to Mama Berta's house, she would stand in front of the painting for a good while to admire it.

It was a huge piece of cloth and the picture on it was that of a man, kneeling down in a place which looked like a beautiful forest garden. His face was in agony and drenched in sweat. He was looking up to the sky, with hands clasped together as if he was praying. A few other men were sleeping on the floor, near him. Kike was deeply touched by this picture the first time she saw it and she asked who the praying man was and Mama Berta told her that the picture was called 'Garden of Gethsemane'.

'That was Jesus just before he was crucified,' she said, 'and those men sleeping near him were his disciples, whom he had told to be his watchmen that particular night.'

Kike could not help being amazed at the perfection of the art. It was so real that she sometimes imagined she saw some movement each time she stared at it.

Mama Berta's living-room was spacious, and she made good use of the space. There were eight beautifully carved wooden chairs and a large table carved out of iroko tree, was placed in the middle of the room to serve as a centre table. The living-room led to a long hallway, which in turn led to each of the five bedrooms. Then there was a small wooden door at the end of the corridor that gave access to the back yard, where a gravelled path takes you to the other three buildings.

The second house in the compound, on the left, was where Wuyi, the gardener and his family, lived. It had no porch, just a simple rectangular shaped building with a flat roof. The house had two bedrooms and a fairly large family room. Also like most of the houses in the area, there was a toilet attached to the building in the back yard. However, they all shared Mama Berta's large kitchen, which was at the back of the main house. The third house, which was directly opposite Wuyi's, was the school where the art and craft workshops took place. It was right beside a deep well, which provided water for the household. The last house in the compound was Mama Berta's cloth-weaving factory. It was at the far end of the compound, backing the rest of her five-acre land.

When Kike and her mum arrived at Mama Berta's that day, she took them to the art and craft school to show them what other teenagers where learning. First they stopped by the well, where two girls were making tie dye. Kike was fascinated by the swiftness at which they worked on the patterns they were making.

'These girls came here about three months ago, with no prior knowledge of how to do tie dye, but look at them now. One would have thought they've been doing it all their lives. They have now learnt how to create beautiful patterns so professionally that they have started selling some of their work. Now they are learning marketing skills,' Mama Berta said, proudly showing off her students.

Kike smiled and said, 'The patterns are lovely and sophisticated.'

Mama Berta smiled and nodded in agreement. She was all the while watching Kike to see if she was keen, but she could see that, although she appreciated the work, she wasn't going to choose that particular art. Mama Berta then took them indoors to see the other craft workshops. She proudly introduced the craft tutor, a man called Ladepo, to her guests, before showing them round the room. Ladepo had his own masonry and raffia-weaving business, but he also taught part-time in Mama Berta's craft school, once a week. Kike and her mum watched as he skilfully wove raffia, with great precision and dexterity.

Mama Berta moved closer to her guests and whispered, 'That man is a very enthusiastic tutor and he has a lot to give to his students. His love for this type of work is contagious.' She then held Kike's hand, pointed to some of the finished products, and then to the students, showing her the process it took to make the beautiful mats hanging on the wall. Kike nodded, but the look on her face was enough to show that she was not too keen on raffia-weaving.

'Let me show you something else,' said their hostess. 'Come with me to the hair-braiding room.' She then led her guests to another room where two girls were waiting patiently.

'Hello, girls,' their tutor greeted cheerfully. 'Have you been waiting for long?'

'No,' they said, shaking their heads. Both of them were 14 years old. Kike watched as Mama Berta began to lay out equipment, in readiness for the day's work. 'That girl inspired me to add hair braiding to my workshops,' she said, pointing to one of the students. 'She was orphaned at the tender age of three and our meeting was a dramatic one. One Saturday morning, I was feeling very low. You see, sometimes I look at everything that God has blessed me with and though I am thankful and I count myself lucky to have such gifts, it still saddens me that I have no child of my own.

So that day, as I sat down to plait my hair into single braids just to keep it tidy, I began to wonder what it would have been like to have had a daughter whose hair I could braid. That was when I began to feel angry.

'I then decided to take a walk to the riverside so as not to give the devil a chance to stretch his ugly hand over my soul. As they say, an idle brain is the devil's workshop. One thing I always do when I feel sad is to go out and look for someone whose situation is worse than mine and bless them that day. That is the only way I get my joy back, apart from praying. 'However, on this particular day, I didn't even feel like praying because I was just too sad.

When I got to the brook, I saw this girl, who was about ten years old at the time. She was washing her grandmother's clothes by the river. Her clothes were all tattered and her hair, goodness! it was in a terrible state. I went to her and we started talking. She told me her name and where she lived and I told her I would pay her a visit that evening.

'I took some food to her house later that day, and I asked if her grandmother wanted her to visit me so I could plait her hair. I would have adopted her, but the old woman understandably refused. She said she was advancing in years and her granddaughter was her only source of joy. I however asked for her permission to help the little girl in any way I could, and she agreed. Since then, this girl has been coming to me every week, to do her hair. She also helps me with some housework for which she gets some pocket money. Helping her has given me a new lease of life.'

By now, Mama Berta had finished setting out the tools on a nearby table. There was a big wooden comb, a smaller one, with a pointed edge for sectioning hair, and a jar of sweet-smelling coconut oil, for dressing the hair.

Just then, a girl came in through the door. She greeted everyone and sat down on one of the chairs. 'Our model is here,' Mama Berta announced. The girl took off the brown scarf that she wearing to cover her hair, and she began to comb her hair.

'Today we are going to learn "pineapple" sectioning,' Mama Berta announced. She took the small sectioning comb and tilted the model's head forward. Then, starting from the nape of her neck, she began sectioning beautiful circular shapes. She then held the rest of the hair back skilfully with the big comb.

Kike was enthralled. How does she do that? She questioned in her mind as she watched the tutor work on the model's hair.

Mama Berta went on to divide each section roughly into three. Then she braided the hair skilfully from the root to the tip and then wrapped it round clockwise into a style called Nubian Knot. As she worked on the hair, the two trainees watched her keenly. After a while, Mama Berta stopped plaiting and asked them to have a go at braiding the rest of the hair, following the method she had used. These they did and the finished style was stunning. The entire scalp looked like a space filled with tessellating diamond shapes.

'I want to learn how to braid,' Kike finally announced.

'Oh, thank God!' said Aduni jubilantly. 'At last she found something she likes. I was beginning to think she wasn't going to be interested in any of the crafts. You know, Kike has a mind of her own. If she doesn't find anything that interests her, she wouldn't choose anything just to make people feel happy.'

'Let her come and start next week then,' said Mama Berta. 'Hair-braiding workshop is held here once a week.'

'How much are we to pay for her tuition?' Aduni asked.

'I do these workshops free of charge,' said Mama Berta. 'I am sowing into these children's lives. My reward would be to see them use the skills they have learnt here and create for themselves an enviable future.'

Aduni was too stunned to say anything.

'The only thing Kike will need is her braiding kit, which should consist of a big wooden comb, ilari, which is the sectioning comb that I used a while ago, and a jar of hair oil.'

'Thank you very much and I pray you won't find it too difficult to teach my daughter. I can see she is captivated by this art and I know she'll be a good student.'

'Come, Kike,' said Aduni, beckoning to her daughter, who was already practising on one of the other students.

'Let her finish the one she is doing and then you are free to take her home,' said Mama Berta.

Back home, Jakobu was waiting eagerly for his wife and daughter.

'You're early today,' said Aduni to him as she and her daughter came into the house.

'Yes, my friend came to help me with harvesting today, and from the look of things, we might have a bountiful produce this year,' he said merrily.

'Congratulations!' said Aduni, with a cheerful smile. She gave her husband a pat on the back, and said, 'I knew you made the right decision to start farming and I am confident that you'll be successful.'

'Thank you, my love. I don't think I could have done it without your support though. You have been such a good wife to me and a good mother to Kike. Our elders say that it is adversity that makes you know the strong and the feeble. Many women would have fallen apart if hit by such terrible storms as have struck our home in the last few years, but you have been there for this family like a solid rock, I am most grateful to you.'

Aduni smiled shyly as she made her way to the kitchen. From the corner of her eyes, she caught her husband looking at her lovingly. Jakobu knows how to make a woman feel wanted, she thought. Aduni felt secure in her husband's love. Her mind was cast back to her wedding night. When Jakobu discovered she had kept herself pure as she had earlier professed, he vowed to remain faithful to her and love her forever. 'I make an oath, never to be unfaithful to you all the days of my life. I am honoured to be the first man to be presented with such an honourable vessel and I will cherish you till the day my body is covered with sand,' he had promised her.

Aduni knew that was not a vain promise and she trusted her husband even when he was miles away from home. As she fetched the wood to cook dinner that night, she remembered the words of her own mother, which were the foundation for her chastity. 'One of the benefits of keeping yourself pure till your wedding night is the honour you receive from your husband,' Mama used to say. 'When a man finds a woman intact, he holds her in high esteem. You see, we live in a cause-and-effect world and whatever you sow you shall reap. If you throw yourself at men like a street dog, you get a pig for a husband. One way or another, loose women attract the scum of the earth and they are treated like second-hand properties.'

Mother's words were usually powerful, Aduni recalled. She was an expert in painting emotional word pictures and she never minced words with anyone. 'Honour your body,' she always said, 'you are God's own temple.'

Aduni sighed, how sad that I will not be able to teach my own daughter these valuable morals, so that she won't give in to the deceits of some men who are only out to take advantage of innocent girls. Now that she is deaf, how will I be able to communicate these essential principles to her? she wondered.

In spite of her deep sadness, Aduni had the assurance that Kike would be fine. She knew her daughter was an emotionally balanced girl.

'Kike isn't the type of girl who would debase herself over sweet nothings. She is a confident child, who knows what she wants in life. My prayer is that these trials won't bring her spirit down,' said Aduni to herself.

'Did Kike find something she is interested in learning today?' Jakobu asked after dinner.

'Yes, she has opted for hair braiding,'

'Hair braiding! What is she going do with hair braiding?' Jakobu could hardly believe what he was hearing.

'You know your daughter, she will only do what she knows she'll enjoy. I don't think we should discourage her though, she has been through such a rough time and the fact that she's even willing to do anything is praiseworthy. I haven't seen any deaf person in this village that has done anything more than beg for money by the roadside.'

'I think you're right in saying that,' Jakobu reasoned. 'Many times I have wondered how it would ever be possible for her to live an independent life. I was overwhelmed with joy when you said Mama Berta agreed to take her on as one of her students. But how on earth is she going to teach a deaf child?'

'I don't know,' replied Aduni, 'but one thing is sure, our elders say that God doesn't make you bald without compensating you with a beard. There's always a blessing in disguise even in the most terrible situations. I think Mama Berta has been sent to us by God, to act as a soothing ointment to our stinging wound. If not for her I don't know what I would have done with myself.'

'You are right, my wife. Even though tears tarry for a night, there is joy in the morning. Although darkness still looms around us, I can see rays of hope penetrating the gloom, you know, like light in the midst of darkness. Mama Berta is remarkable and she has such strong faith. The only strange thing is that she doesn't worship any of our gods like Ogun, Ifa, and so on. What did you say her religion is?'

'She says she believes in God, known by her mother's tribe as Yahweh, and his son Jesu Kristi.'

'Jesu Kristi? Who is this Jesu Kristi? Is he an Ethiopian god of some sort?' Jakobu wanted to know.

'I don't know too much about the religion but she said the worship of Yahweh came into Ethiopia through Queen Sheba. She said during one of the queen's travels she met a great king called Solomon in one of the countries in the Middle East, and the queen heard many extraordinary stories during her visit to this land. She herself witnessed the wisdom with which King Solomon ruled his people and she became converted. When she came back to her own kingdom, she shared the story with all her courtiers and many of them were also converted.'

'Really?' said Jakobu, who was listening intently.

'Mama Berta also said that many years after, during the reign of the great Ethiopian Queen, Candace, a remarkable thing happened. One of the palace eunuchs, a man of great authority, went to Jerusalem for the yearly worship. There he met an evangelist called Phillip. The eunuch asked Phillip to explain some verses in the holy book to him. He'd been reading this passage but he couldn't understand it. He was reading about a man who was slaughtered like a lamb by his own people.

'Phillip then explained to him that the man he was reading about was Jesu Kristi and that this man is the son of God. He was crucified but he had risen up and he lives forever. Anyone who wants to worship God from then on would do it through this Jesu. The eunuch came back to the palace with this new knowledge and that was how Ethiopia became one of the first African countries to embrace this faith.'

'Amazing story,' said Jakobu. 'I would like to know more. I think we should attend one of her meetings one day, I am sure she'd explain more to us.'

The following week, Kike went to start her training. Mama Berta divided the hair-braiding course into two stages. The first was introduction to braids whereby the girls learnt about grooming hair before plaiting. The second stage was hair sectioning, three-strand and two-strand plaits.

Kike was determined to be the best in her class. Mama Berta has been so good to me, she thought, I even owe my life to her. I can still vividly recall how she and Tito's mother had brought me back to consciousness the day I fainted. I want her to be proud of me, so I'll try my utmost to complete this training successfully, she promised herself.

She watched with rapt attention every time Mama Berta did a demonstration, so that she could repeat what she'd been taught with little or no mistakes. Her tutor was also extra-gentle with her and she went through every instruction carefully until Kike understood each process perfectly.

One day, Mama Berta was explaining to her students how to identify different types of hair. 'Some people's hair feels spongy; some have very tight curls, while some are wavy. 'We also have the thin, lightweight hair. It is important to identify hair texture first, before deciding on the style you want to plait. Some styles will enhance thick hair, but would look ridiculous when worn by anyone with thin hair.'

As Mama Berta spoke, she noticed that Kike looked confused and disorientated. 'Poor child,' she said, 'you can't even hear a word of what I've been saying.' She also noticed that Kike still maintained eye contact with people just like a hearing person would. Mama Berta watched Kike keenly and a thought flashed through her mind. I think if this child can watch people's mouths, she might be able to understand a bit, even if not all what people are saying. Thank God she was not born deaf. She's heard people speak before so it shouldn't be too difficult for her to lip-read.

She beckoned to Kike to come to her front room. 'Look here,' she said to her, and she pointed to Kike's eyes with her right hand and touched her lips with her left. 'Watch my lips and see if you can grasp some of what I am saying.'

'What is your name?' she asked, wanting to start with something simple. She spoke slowly and repeated her question twice.

Kike beamed, as she understood what her tutor was trying to teach her. 'My name is Kike.'

114

'Okay, what is your mother's name?'

'Aduni,' she responded.

'Go and bring me some water,' said Mama Berta, happy that she was getting somewhere with her young student.

Kike went to the kitchen and reappeared with a bowl of water.

They were together practising lip-reading for the next one and a half hours. Some of the words were difficult for Kike, but she persevered. Her tutor gently explained to her that from that day she mustn't look at people's eyes when she was listening to them. She must always face people and watch their mouths as they spoke.

'You need that for your survival, my child,' she said, patting her on the head. She had grown so fond of Kike, since her illness. She secretly hoped that one day Kike would be healed of her deafness, and she remembered her in her prayers every night. 'I am not going to give up on you, my baby. You are still going to hear me again,' she said.

Kike could not wait to get home to tell her parents about the lip-reading. Unfortunately, her mum was not in when she arrived home and her father was taking a nap. She then went to the back yard to pluck some ripe mangoes as it was mango season.

She looked across the yard to Tito's compound and saw a group of women dancing and singing. What is happening at our neighbour's? she wondered. Then she remembered it was ritual day for Tito's twins. It was Taiwo and Kehinde's fourteenth birthday and their mum always celebrated their birthday in a special way. She always cooked a special type of beans called 'ewa ibeji.' Then she would invite her family and friends to her house for a party.

Kike continued to watch as the women danced joyfully round the twins. They had formed a circle round the two boys. 'I bet I know the song they are singing,' she said. Just then a thought came to her mind. Why don't I put my lip-reading into practice? She moved closer to Tito's back yard and fixed her gaze on one of the women, who appeared to be the leader of the dancers.

'Amazing!' said Kike excitedly. 'This thing works.' She watched the woman keenly and found that truly she could read her lips.

They were singing the traditional 'twins ritual song' called 'Epo mbe'.

Epo mbe, ewa mbe o [There is palm oil and there is beans]
Aya mi o ja Oo ee [I am not afraid Oo ee]
Aya mi o ja lati bi 'beji [I am not afraid to give birth to twins]
Epo mbe, ewa mbe o [There is palm oil and there is beans].

The women danced beautifully. The twins were obviously extremely shy. They used to enjoy the ceremony when they were little and they loved the attention and the food, but now they saw the whole ceremony as unnecessary.

'Are we going to continue dancing with Mother like this all the rest of our lives?' asked Taiwo, the first of the twins.

'I don't know,' Kehinde answered. Then he added fearfully, 'I sure hope not, because it's getting too embarrassing for me, standing in the midst of all these women.'

Taiwo laughed.

'You think it's funny,' said Kehinde scowling at his brother. 'Wait till you start dating a girl and mother drags you to dance "epo mbe" right in front of your girlfriend. That is my own worst fear – I don't know about you.'

'I'm not afraid of anything,' said Taiwo, who was the more boisterous of the two. 'If mother calls me to dance "epo mbe" in front of my girlfriend, I'll run away from home.'

'Aha, see how foolish you are, big mouth,' said his twin brother rudely.' And what do you think mother would do, eh? Before you ever get to the village border, she'll have touts on you, and they'll drag you back to the village by your ears.'

At that moment, Kehinde caught sight of Kike staring at them. 'What on earth is she doing there?' he asked angrily

'Who?'

'That deaf girl next door.'

'You mean Kike?'

'Yes, see how she's staring at us as if we are aliens.'

'She means no harm, ignore her,' said Taiwo reassuringly.

Kike was carried away by her newly found independence. She was lip-reading the twins and didn't realise she was staring at them in the process. Then she saw Kehinde pointing at her. She quickly got up from where she was and ran indoors.

117

Chapter 9

HIDDEN TREASURES REVEALED

IT was Kike's graduation day. She woke up early, sat on her mat and said her early-morning prayers just as her tutor had taught her. Altogether, she had spent seven months at Mama Berta's training school and she had learnt a lot during the period, this included; grooming hair for plaiting; various sectioning patterns for three-strand and two-strand plaits; hair adornment for special occasions and a lot about after-care for braids.

That morning however, Kike could not explain the niggling feeling of sorrow she had. 'I don't know why I am so sad,' she said to herself. 'This is supposed to be my day of joy. My mother is over the moon, Father even took the day off work just to rejoice with me, yet I feel so miserable.'

She began to think about the events of the past five years. Her sickness started when she was only ten years old. At that time, the only thing she wanted to do was tell stories, play the djembe drum and travel around the world. She felt the illness had changed the course of her destiny. Tears were beginning to cloud her vision. She was getting more and more despondent and she began to cry.

After a while she stopped crying and wiped her face with the back of her hand. 'Why am I crying on a day like this? I am meant to be happy, not sad.' Unfortunately she could not hold back tears. They continued to flow ceaselessly, like a stream that suddenly overflowed its bank, tearing down all the barriers.

After what seemed like ages, Kike went to the bathroom to clean up. Later, she got out the new cloth her mum had got her for the graduation ceremony. It was a beautiful multicoloured fabric, with the picture of two women dancers printed on it. She took another look at the picture on the fabric and began to cry again.

'Now, Kike, this is stupid. Calm down and get ready for your big day,' she told herself. 'After all, I am only fifteen years old. I have a whole life ahead of me to do what I want. This self-pity has to stop right now or I'll spoil the day for my dear parents and Mama Berta, who have spent so much time and energy to see me get to where I am today.'

Kike then sat down to think about the style she would plait at the graduation ceremony later in the day. The event would be at Mama Berta's house, after which the graduates were expected to take their guests to their own homes for entertainment. At the ceremony, the girls would create a style that they had never done before and judges would be there to award prizes. I will plait *moramo* (spiral). I have practised it on Tito's daughter and it looked quite good, although I have to work faster today, she mused.

About an hour later, Aduni woke up to clean up the house, but first she went to her daughter's room.

'Kike, you are up early, I knew the excitement wouldn't let you sleep.' She patted her on the head like she used to do when she was a little girl. 'I am really proud of you, my child. What our enemies planned for evil, God has turned it round for good. They thought you would end up on the streets begging for money, but today you are going to stand tall in the presence of your enemies who have brought this calamity to you and you will declare to them that whoever God has not debased, no one else can.' Aduni obviously strongly believed that some witches had cast a spell on her daughter, which was what caused her deafness.

Although Aduni knew her daughter could not hear her, she still continued. 'My child, you shall live long to see the demise of your enemies, and you will continue to increase while they decrease.'

'Thank you, mother,' said Kike, who already knew it was going to be an emotional day for her parents, especially her mum.

'Mother, why don't you start getting ready while I get dressed?'

'Good idea, I'll go and wake your father up, and then I'll prepare breakfast.'

Later that morning, they all converged at Mama Berta's for the graduation ceremony and there were lots of people there. Kike came second at the competition and she got a set of four wooden hair adornments. After the ceremony, Aduni invited people to her house for a celebration party.

Her friend Yemi and a group of other women had been cooking all morning – there was pounded yam with egusi soup; gari with okra soup and red stew; fufu and goat-meat soup and other side dishes like fried plantain and steamed beans. Jakobu had ordered fresh palm wine from Oto, the village palm-wine taper, the night before, and it was frothing in large gourds in one corner.

Mama Berta had to honour the invitation of all her students but she decided to come to Kike's house last so she could stay there all evening. She brought along bata and gangan drummers and a group of village dancers to make the party merrier.

Kike refused to dance because she could not hear the music, and she would not make a fool of herself. However, she drank a lot of palm wine until she began to get tipsy.

'That is enough palm wine, young woman,' said her mother when Kike went for her fourth round. 'How many women have you seen gulping down alcohol the way you are doing? I certainly hope you are not going to take after your father. His weakness is that moocher in the gourd. Look at him – he is drunk already and the party hasn't even started.' Jakobu was dancing and singing loudly with his friends. As he hopped and skipped, he threw his cap to the sky and tried to catch it with his chest. He looked extremely silly but he wasn't bothered, he was intoxicated.

Kike took one look at her dad, and she needed no convincing. She left her calabash near the man serving the palm wine and went to thank everyone who had come to celebrate with her. People hugged her and some patted her back. Many of them had come to the party out of curiosity to see a deaf girl who was becoming successful. That was the first time in the history of their village that a person with a disability did something worthwhile.

121

Kike however, believed that part of the problem faced by people with disabilities, especially the deaf, was that no one knew how to communicate with them, so they were ignored and treated like they had contagious diseases. Lack of communication and human contact made them secluded, hence frustrated, and many times they threw tantrums, especially the younger ones. Therefore, they were labelled headstrong and violent.

The party at Kike's house continued till dawn the next day. It was a successful event, which was the talk of the village many months after. This brought Kike a lot of fame. Parents with wayward children could be heard calling their children to caution and saying things like, 'If Kike, who is deaf, can make headway in life, why can't you?'

One day, Jumoke, one of Kike's childhood friends, was having a heated argument with her mother, and in anger her mum said to her, 'Look at Kike, the girl you grew up with. She was unfortunate to contract an incurable disease which left her deaf, but see where she is today. Isn't it such a pity that those who have cap have no head and those who have heads have no cap?' By this she meant that Kike still managed to do well in spite of all odds while those who had no disability could not be bothered.

Apparently, Jumoke's mum had paid a lot of money for her daughter to be an apprentice to a local fabric maker, but the girl never went there. She was too busy playing the 'popular with the boys.' She got pregnant just before her sixteenth birthday, and no one knew who the father was.

A few months after Kike's graduation, her parents invited Mama Berta to their home to discuss Kike's future. It wasn't that Kike didn't know what she wanted but her parents still found it somewhat difficult to communicate with her effectively. They relied so much on Mama Berta's help and they often sent for her, when they needed to discuss anything important concerning Kike.

'I would like Father to find me a plot of land and help me build a shop,' Kike announced when everyone was seated. 'I want to set up a hair-braiding salon.'

Aduni turned to Mama Berta and said, 'I have never heard of a hair-braiding salon, no one round here goes to anyone to plait their hair, not to mention paying to have it done.'

Mama Berta knew Kike was trying to lip-read her, so she spoke slowly. You are right Aduni, but that is because people don't know much about hair plaiting. Most people round here either cut theirs short and those who have long hair comb it out, and tie it into a bun or cover it with a scarf. It's only on special occasions that some people manage to braid their hair into two or three single plaits. Even so they still rub animal fat on it and decorate it with beads and woven bands. Did you not see how the audience applauded when my students did those intricate designs on their graduation? Since then, up to a dozen people have stopped me on the street, asking if any of my girls could plait their hair either into tiny three-strand or two-strand plaits.'

'Yes, but would that be enough for her to make a living?' argued Aduni. 'This is something no one else has ever done. Is that not too much of a risk? Why can't she open a shop and sell cloths, artefacts and other things like most other girls round here do?'

Kike could pick out a few words from what her mother was saying and she was becoming angry. Lately, she seemed not to be able to tolerate anybody. She fumed and ranted at the slightest wrong anyone did to her. It was as if she was getting shorter tempered by the day. This was one of the reasons her parents always called her tutor whenever they needed to have important discussions such as the one they were having that day.

Mama Berta listened attentively before addressing Kike. 'I perceive you got the gist of what your mother just said, what have you to say?'

Kike was silent.

'Talk to me, it's rude to ignore your elders.'

Still Kike would not say a word.

Then Mama Berta feigned anger. She banged the table in front of her and stood up as if ready to go. 'When you are ready to say something you know where I am.'

Thinking her guest was truly angry Aduni grabbed her hand, and began to plead with her. 'Please don't go, if you leave now, who'll help us sort this out? Please try to understand Kike, she is not intentionally rude, she has a lot of resentment piled up in her and rather than deal with it, she lets it out on people who are close to her.'

Then, just as Mama Berta was about to sit down again, Kike got up, stormed out of the room and began to shout, 'Is it not bad enough that fate has brought my dream of becoming a storyteller to a halt, now my parents are trying to put a stumbling block in my way. I said I want to open a braiding salon, they are asking me to sell cloths. If I wanted to sell cloths would I have spent nearly a year learning hair braiding?'

Then she hissed very loudly, which threw Jakobu totally off balance. He got up angrily and followed Kike to her room and then gave her a slap across her face. That was the first time in several years anyone did that to Kike. In fact she could hardly remember the last time she was smacked.

Kike held her right cheek and began to cry. She was literally shouting at the top of her voice. She did not know which hurt her most, the pain from the slap or the fact that her father had slapped her.

Jakobu raised his finger to his mouth and said, 'Shut up, young woman, or you'll get a second helping! I think you're becoming a selfish fool. You've been rude to us many times and we've stomached it, thinking it is because of your condition. We, your parents, can hardly say anything to you without having a third party nearby just in case you throw one of your tantrums. As if all that is not enough, you have the audacity to be rude to our guest. Your mother was even apologising on your behalf and the next thing is for you to walk out on us, hissing all the way like a snake. My mother would turn in her grave to see a child treat her parents thus.' Jakobu ranted on and on as if Kike could hear what he was saying. He was obviously extremely angry. 'I have tolerated your insolence enough. You are becoming spoilt to stinking level!' he yelled.

He then grabbed his daughter by her shoulder and turned her to face him. 'Listen to me, girl, you are going back to the front room and you're going to apologise to those two women who helped you get to where you are today.' As he spoke, he pointed to the front room where Mama Berta and his wife were, and he made a gesture to show Kike what to do. 'Do you understand me?' he asked.

Kike nodded. She was sad and embarrassed. However, the look on her father's face made her realise he wasn't going to tolerate any nonsense. She quickly made her way to the front room and went on her knees the customary way, to ask Mama Berta and her mother for forgiveness, and then she went into her bedroom. Aduni was upset as well as perplexed. She

124

did not know who to vent her anger on. She didn't like the way Kike behaved, at the same time she hated her husband for inflicting pain on their daughter by slapping her.

Aduni's face was a sight to behold. Whenever she was angry, she pressed her lips together until they formed a straight hard line. The menacing frown on her face made her eyes look like they were holding a horsewhip, ready to lash out at any moment.

Mama Berta could sense the tension. 'Would you like to go with me to see my new building site? I need to see how the roofing is going on.'

Before Aduni could answer, Jakobu cut in and said, 'I am going to play ayo with my friends at the village square and I'll see you all later.' He took his cap from the table and as he was about to leave, Aduni called out to him.

'Do me a favour, Jakobu, kindly bring home the dregs of the palm wine you drown your sorrow in, so I can drown mine in it as well.'

Jakobu shook his head and left without saying a word.

Silence followed.

After what seemed like five minutes, Mama Berta said, 'We don't have to go to my building site if you don't want to.'

Aduni did not answer. She simply sat there, arms folded across her chest, sulking like a little girl.

'I am very sorry about the whole situation,' said Mama Berta. 'I feel responsible for all this, because if I hadn't feigned anger earlier and pretended I was going, all this would not have happened. I underestimated the way Kike is feeling and I am so sorry that a meeting, which was meant for good, should end like this.'

Aduni began to cry. 'It is not your fault, believe me. It is nobody's fault. I don't seem to understand anything any more. I am tired, weary, fed up and I just feel like running away. I want to go to a place of rest and tranquillity. I don't seem to be doing anything right, as you can see.'

Mama Berta held Aduni's hands and squeezed them firmly. 'Listen to me, my child, you have done very well. I don't know many women who would not have had a nervous breakdown going through the same adversities as you.'

'Maybe I am about to have a nervous breakdown myself.'

'Don't say such things, Aduni! Words are powerful,' Mama Berta rebuked.

Silence ensued again and then Aduni asked, 'Why did Jakobu slap Kike? How could he be so cruel and insensitive? I know my daughter has not been the best person to be with lately, but she is hardly herself. Only God knows what goes on in her head, locked up in her own silent world. Is that not enough to make anyone go mad?'

Mama Berta remained hushed. She knew Aduni was suffering and she needed to talk. Aduni continued to pour out her heart to this kind and gentle lady who gave her undivided attention. When Aduni eventually stopped talking, Mama Berta sat up straight and said, 'Listen, I cannot say I feel what you are feeling right now because I am not in your situation, but, believe me, I do sympathise with you. I want you to give me your attention, because I am about to tell you things about myself that I have not shared with anyone in this village up till now.

'First, I want to beg you not to be too hard on Jakobu. He loves Kike as much as you do and he wants what is best for her. You see, I grew up in a family where my father was the disciplinarian but my mother was weak in the area of discipline and she tolerated a lot of bad behaviour. She tried her best to let us know right from wrong but that was not enough. You see, it is one thing to inform your children about what to do but it is another to make sure they carry out instructions. Unfortunately, my father was away a lot, which made matters worse.

'To cut a long story short, when I was growing up, I knew what was expected of me, as regards my relationship with men, but I went in the other direction and I paid for it dearly later in my life. When I was a teenager, I met this young man in Ibadan where I lived before coming to this village. He was a very handsome man, smooth and eloquent with words and he had his way with young girls. I knew he had chains of girlfriends and they all worshipped the ground he walked on, yet I was so flattered that he took interest in me and I wasn't bothered about his reputation, so I started going out with him. One of the neighbours alerted my mother who later asked me if it was true that I was going out with this loser. I told her I loved the man and my mother never said anything about it again.

'Two years went by and one day, this man told me he didn't want to have anything to do with me again. I was heartbroken and I nearly killed myself. Shortly after he left me, I started having sharp pains in my abdomen, which resulted in my being very ill, and I was bedridden for about five weeks. First my mother thought I was pregnant but after about six months and no sign of pregnancy, she believed me. I became well again and I began going out with another man who was married. I don't know why I attracted such men to my life. This man, unlike my first boyfriend, was ugly and scruffy-looking. Our relationship was mainly physical. In fact people hardly saw us together, mainly because he was married anyway and also because he was not presentable and I knew my friends would laugh at me.

'One day, as I was coming back from the brook where I went to wash my clothes I felt the old pain again, only this time it was so severe I passed out. When the pain did not subside, a friend of mine took me to see an old woman who lived in a neighbouring village, a few miles from Ibadan. The woman was an herbalist. She asked me a lot of questions, which I answered to the best of my knowledge. I also described the pain to her and she began to examine me. She continually shook her head, as she continued the examination, which was slow, painful and degrading to say the least.

'When she finished, she paused for a while and said to me, "Child, you have a severe form of venereal disease. I don't know what type it is, but this I can tell you, it has destroyed your organs so much that you don't even have a womb any more!" Her words were like a horsewhip on a bare back.

'"Witch! it is your daughter who would have no womb," I swore at her under my breath. Then I beckoned to my friend that I was going and I left the woman's hut without even saying a word of thanks. I wasn't ready to listen to such nonsense anymore. My friend quickly paid the woman and ran after me.

'"That was very rude," she exploded when she had caught up with me. "After all, we were the ones that came to see her, she did not send for us."

'"Did you hear all the rubbish she said?" I asked my friend.

'"She may be right, you know," my friend answered.

'I eyed my friend, hissed and told her I never wanted to see her again and I ran all the way home. I was so frightened. Ever heard of a woman with no womb? "How on earth would I be able to conceive a child?" I asked myself. However, I told no one about the incident, not even my mother.

'About three years later, I got married and for several years we tried for a child to no avail. My worst nightmare had come to haunt me. I knew my husband and I had no children because of me. So it was true what that old woman had said. The guilt I carried became so unbearable that one night I told my husband the entire story of my life. Hitherto, he'd thought he was married to a saint and I had allowed him to believe that for many years. "What you don't know does not hurt you," was my theory. However, I was sick of living a lie, which led me eventually to come clean, though I knew it was a great risk.

Unfortunately, I was not prepared for my husband's reaction. He was obviously shocked and even left the house for about two weeks. When he came back, things went from bad to worse. Six months after, he began seeing another woman and he eventually told me to leave. He then married his bride and they had their first child some months after. Although I begged him not to tell anyone about my past, I am sure he must have told his new wife.

'The shame was too much to live with. People stared at me on the streets, in the market and so on. I had to leave my home town and that was how I came to Aje.' At this point, Mama Berta sighed sorrowfully and said, 'that is the story of my life.'

Aduni was horrified. She sat there staring at her guest. Her mouth was wide open but no words came out.

'Is it true, all you've been saying?' she managed to ask when she had gathered herself together.

'The whole truth,' replied Mama Berta. 'Hard to believe but it is the truth.'

'But I'd always thought…'Aduni could not continue.

'Thought I was a saint as well?' the elderly woman teased.

'No, not that,' Aduni protested, 'it's just that em…em…' She was lost for words.

'Well, Aduni, things aren't always what they seem. I have a past that I am ashamed of, but I was given a second chance and that is why you see me doing all I can to support our youth, especially the young girls. It is so easy for them to fall into the trap of seeking approval and attention from men.

'You see, when you love your children unconditionally, you are giving them a solid foundation, which should act as a launch pad in their journey to fulfil their destiny. Also, when you believe in them, encourage and support them to make good choices and right decisions, then you are giving them wings with which to fly and not even the sky is their limit. However, discipline is an essential part of unconditional love. As much as I am against cruelty to children, yet I am of the opinion that parents who shy away from disciplining their children, or those that do not stick to their guns and make sure their offspring obey instructions, do not really care about them. Some parents think gifts and pampering alone buys love. Nothing is further from the truth.

'When I was young, I did not like the way my father disciplined us, yet I loved him, and looking back now I appreciate the little he was able to do for us. However, my mother feared she might lose us if she was too hard on us, but then, as a young girl, I did not understand that her seemingly carefree attitude was motivated by fear. I just thought she couldn't be bothered and that she didn't care. This led me to seek love and approval from men, and I fell into the wrong hands. This is why I said to you, earlier on, never be frightened of correcting your child or disciplining her – it would be for her own good and she will definitely thank you for it later.'

Aduni got up and gave Mama Berta a warm hug. 'Thank you very much,' she said. 'You have always been a source of inspiration to me, and thank you for sharing that story with me. It must have been so painful for you to reveal all that but I can assure you, I will not babble this to anyone. I would like to know how you were able to get your life back to normal though,' she added.

'Well, just before I came here to live, I took a trip to Ethiopia, my mother's country. There, I met a woman who first taught me how to read and then gave me a bible, which I read day and night. In this book, I learnt some basic principles that helped me start afresh. I also learnt about genuine love, and how to forgive myself and others. Then, I began to

experience peace that surpasses all understanding. The kind of peace you experience even when you are in a tempest. It is from this same book that I share words of wisdom every week at those meetings, and the feedback I get from people who attend is phenomenal. However, that is another long story, let's save it for another day. By the way, where is Kike?'

'I saw her going out while we were talking. I think she has gone for a walk.'

'Tell her to come and see me tomorrow,' said Mama Berta on her way out.

Meanwhile, Kike had gone to her sacred spot. This was the corn field, where she had the strange dream some months back. Every time she was troubled, she found solace there.

She lay there for a while, thinking about the events of the day. She felt really bad that she had upset her parents and her dear tutor. She was also angry that her father had slapped her and as she recalled the whole incident again, tears trickled down her cheeks. Here she was, a girl who had bright hopes for her future, but the hand of fate snatched her dreams and aspirations from her. Refusing to give up, she found an alternative, but now even the alternative was slipping out of her hands gradually. She had worked very hard, the past seven months trying to learn a trade she liked. She thought her parents would jump for joy immediately she announced that she wanted a shop of her own, but alas, nothing in life is easy.

Maybe I should have got myself a corner in the market place and begged for alms. That would really have been a lot easier to do, she thought. Then, I wouldn't have a single heartache, no struggles, only wake up, have a wash, then go out and bask in the pity and gifts of passers-by.

Just then, the wind began to blow lightly, rustling the leaves on nearby trees. Strangely, it seemed as if her inner mind picked up a gentle still small voice amidst the rustlings, saying to her, 'You do not need anyone to teach you anything because your spirit knows all things.' Kike looked around to see if anyone was there but she saw no one.

Where had she heard those words before?

Aha! It was from Paul, the man she saw in her dream a while ago. She began to ponder on these words. This shifted her attention from the negative thoughts that were beginning to envelop her mind.

She got up from the corn field and made her way back home. On the way, she saw a field that had tall elephant grass. Kike loved elephant grasses. She liked to pull and tug at them and although they sometimes made her body itch, she still enjoyed rolling in them. She ran to the field and began pulling the grass. She took a handful and divided them into three sections and had fun braiding them. The braids looked beautiful.

Then she marked out a spot and decided to braid all the grass in the area. She did the three-strand plaits successfully and when she saw how beautiful the grass looked, she began to think of how to join the plaits together from the beginning of the row to the end. This, however, proved a bit difficult as she did not know how to join them together. The type of hair braiding she had learnt from Mama Berta were two-strand and three-strand single plaits.

She tried several methods of joining all the plaits to form one single line, but to no avail. Then she began to mutter some positive affirmations, 'I can do all things.' Then she sat down again and divided the elephant grass into three, and she began to plait. However, rather than plait each one to the end, she wove it halfway and added more grass as she went along. She continued to plait the grass this way until she got to the end of the row that she had marked out. The result was astounding. She quickly marked out another section and repeated what she had just done, plaiting backwards and picking more grass as she went along. She wove her way in and out of the blades of grass, and at the end of the line she plaited the remaining to the tip to end it.

Kike then stood back to examine her work. She was stunned. 'How did I do that?' she exclaimed. 'Oh my,' she cried, 'I must do some more.' She was so excited that she forgot that her parents might be getting worried about her. She went back to work on the grass. She plaited and plaited until sunset. Tired and exhausted, she got up and began to jump and clap. She felt like someone who had just received a revelation about some hidden treasure. She knew she had just discovered something extraordinary. At that point in time, she was not sure what she was going to do with her new discovery, but she knew something was going to come out of it.

Kike half-skipped, half-jumped home. She even began to whistle although she couldn't hear herself. She got home just in time for dinner. She smiled at her mother and gave her a hug.

'My child!' was all Aduni could say, obviously touched by Kike's warmth, although unsure of the reason why her daughter was looking so cheerful and merry, after all that had happened earlier on.

'Where have you been?' she asked suspiciously.

Kike, who by then had mastered the art of lip-reading, answered with some gesticulation: 'I have been in the fields plaiting grass.'

'Oh,' said Aduni and she carried on with her work.

Kike was not perturbed by her mother's unenthusiastic response.

In her mind, she had settled on the fact that she was going to pursue a career in hair braiding whether her parents liked it or not.

That night as she lay on her mat, she recalled all that had happened that day.

Where do I go from here? she wondered. Yes, I am excited about my discovery, but what happens next? That night, she had a dream that she plaited the entire grass in the village, which made many people angry, and they tried to chase her out of the village, but a young man in a white robe came to her rescue. Then he gave her a white sheet of paper and the words written on it in gold were:

> "I have more understanding than all my teachers:
> For your testimonies are my meditations."
>
> Psalm 119, verse 99.

Although Kike could neither read nor write, as formal education was not yet in existence in her village at that time, yet, in her dream, she read this beautiful verse and understood it perfectly.

Amazingly, she remembered every word of it when she woke up next morning.

Chapter 10

CORNROW

'IS that you, Aduni?' Jakobu called from the living-room when he heard footsteps.

'Yes, it's me.'

'Welcome, how was market today?' Jakobu asked caringly.

'Well, today is gone, may God keep us safe till another day,' his wife replied.

Whenever Aduni sounded like that, Jakobu knew sales were not too brilliant, so he tried to cheer her up. 'Never mind, as long as there is life there is hope. Actually, I should have gone out but I had to wait for you to come in from the market. There was a message from the chief for Kike.'

'Really?' said Aduni, rushing to him.

'The messenger said that Olori Teju, the chief's senior wife, saw you in the market earlier on, and she was intrigued by your hairstyle. She later made enquiries and she was told it was Kike who braided it.'

'And?' Aduni was getting a bit impatient.

'Well, she wants our daughter to come and plait her hair. She is attending an important meeting next week and she wants to be noticeable among the crowd of women.'

Aduni shouted and clapped loudly. 'Where is Kike?'

'She went out not too long ago, she said she was going to see a man who will rent a shop out to her in the market.'

'So she is still going ahead with her plans to have a hair-braiding salon?'

'Yes, she is, Aduni, and I think we should just leave her alone to get on with her life, and give her our full support and blessing.'

Aduni eyed her husband charily and said, 'Why the sudden change of mind? This time last week, you wouldn't even hear of it.'

Her husband did not reply.

Aduni knew that the message they got from the chief's wife had a lot to do with Jakobu wanting them to support their daughter.

As Aduni got ready to cook dinner, she remembered the day Kike first plaited the new style that she had discovered on her hair. She had never seen her daughter so happy, at least not since her illness started. Her excitement that day was contagious.

That Saturday afternoon, she had groomed her mother's hair ready for plaiting. Hitherto, Kike only knew how to do the single plaits she had learnt from Mama Berta, but that day, instead of the single plaits, she began to section her mum's hair into long rows, from the front hairline to the nape of her neck. She sectioned the first vertical line and held the rest back with a large comb. Then she stood behind her mother and began to weave her hair non-stop from front to back, picking more hair as she went along, just as she did with the grass a few weeks back.

The first one was not very smooth, but she continued to improve on it. She did six rows of hair and when she finished, she stood back to examine the style and gasped in disbelief.

She was beside herself with joy. She half-pulled and half-dragged her mother to the front yard, where Jakobu was playing ayo with his friend, Yomi. She began to shout, 'Look, Father, look!'

Aduni did not know what to make of her daughter's exuberance, because she could not see her hair. So she simply stood there staring at her husband, mouth wide open, hoping to get an explanation from him. Unfortunately, Jakobu was of no help.

'Look at what?' he asked, head buried in his game.

'Papa, look, I say!' Kike insisted.

This time, Jakobu looked up from the game in exasperation.

Kike saw that her father was staring at her and not at her mother, and she began to point at her mother's hair. 'Look, look!' she yelled.

'Oh,' said Jakobu. 'It's beautiful.'

When he saw the disappointed look on her daughter's face, he added, 'It's very beautiful. In fact the most creative thing I've ever seen.' Unfortunately, his words were not backed by action so it was obvious he only said that to get rid of both mother and daughter.

Kike turned to her father's friend, as if to say, 'Help me here.'

'Yes,' said Yomi. 'I agree that it is gorgeous.'

'Is the style different from the ones she's done for me before?' Aduni eventually managed to ask.

Jakobu turned his back so that Kike could not lip-read him. 'I don't know,' he admitted. 'She came in here dragging you along, saying I should look at your hair. Maybe it is a new style she just learnt.'

'Look more closely then!' Aduni shouted angrily. 'That ayo game is not going to disappear, you know. Can you not tell if it is a new style or not?'

'Woman, please leave me alone!' Jakobu snapped back. 'I know nothing about women's hair. In fact I cannot tell between hair that is plaited and one that is not, even if you hold it right up to my nose, ha! ha! ha!' he laughed.

By this time, Yomi, who had held back laughter for so long, also burst out laughing.

Aduni's eyes were gradually turning red. She was fuming with rage as she watched the two men resume their game.

'That game is going to give you your evening meal,' she hollered, 'and warm up your bed tonight,' she added irately and stormed indoors.

'Ouch, my friend, I do not envy you,' Yomi derided, and shook his head from side to side. 'I can smell trouble. Anyway, that's the problem with men like you who stick to one wife. As for me, if one of my wives is angry with me, all I need to do is check in with one of the others. Within a few hours, the angry one will come crawling back, begging.'

Jakobu looked at him in disgust and said, 'That is the way you have chosen to live your life. Each person's lifestyle is different. For me, one wife is more than enough. I haven't even done enough to satisfy Aduni and make her happy, not to mention sharing my meagre resources with another woman. They say one woman, one trouble, two women, two troubles, and on and on it goes.'

By this time Yomi was scowling. However, this did not deter his friend who continued to lash out at him.

'My advice to you, Yomi, is to take care of yourself, you only get one chance to pass through this world. You look haggard and much older than your age, because your house is like a battlefield. Your children hate themselves and they do combat like soldiers from two enemy countries, forced to live together in the same camp. You have no control over your household, and you call that being a man?'

By now Yomi was off his seat, fuming with rage. 'I've just about had enough of you spurting dirt out of the corners of your mouth, pal! What goes on in my family is none of your business. After all, I have never come to you for advice on how to run my home.'

'Some home,' Jakobu sniggered, satisfied to be the one to have the last say. He stood up, stretched his arms and legs and sat down again, beaming with relish.

After a while, Yomi eventually calmed down and he broke the silence.

'In spite of your rudeness, I am still willing to help you,' he said.

'Help me, what do you mean?'

'Yes, help you. Your wife is not going to cook for you tonight, nor warm your bed.'

'So?'

'So you know where my house is, if you need to eat. You don't have to starve to death, ha! ha! ha!'

Jakobu was not amused by this comment, so he quickly changed the subject and said, 'Do you want us to resume this game or would you rather call it a day?'

By now he was no longer smiling.

Aduni came out again to look for Kike, who had left quietly when she sensed that her mother was angry with her father. When Aduni could not find her, she went back indoors and began to examine her hair with her hand. She could not understand how Kike was able to weave her hair to the back non-stop. 'Poor girl,' Aduni muttered. 'This is a style she's never done before, I am sure. No wonder she was so excited. And that Jakobu could not even see beyond his nose.

'Men,' she hissed, 'thank God I am a woman. Sometimes I think men were actually meant to live on another planet.'

After about two hours, Kike came into the house, closely followed by Mama Berta. She went straight to her mother, pointed to her hair and asked, 'What do you think?'

Mama Berta was mesmerised. 'What – how – when? I mean where did you learn this style?' She kept on stumbling on her words.

'Ha! appreciation at last,' Kike smiled as she watched the lady's astonished look.

'I think this is absolutely marvellous,' said Mama Berta, eventually recovering from her shock.

'What exactly did she do with my hair?' asked Aduni who was still not able to take in all the excitement happening around her.

'I can't explain it, but I'll try.' She moved closer to Aduni to examine her hair and as she ran her hand through it, she began to give details of how the hair was done.

'You see, she sectioned the hair into straight lines, instead of the circular or triangular shapes you do for single plaits, and then she did a continuous weave, picking more hair as she went along, until she came to the end of the line. What I don't know is where she got this idea from or who taught her. I haven't seen anything like this before.' She then turned to face Kike and asked, 'Where did you learn this?'

After Kike had grasped her question, she pointed to herself. 'I taught myself with long elephant grass.' She then went on to narrate the story about the day she discovered how to plait the new style, while playing with elephant grass.

'Amazing!' said Mama Berta, still short of words. 'Would you like to do my hair when you are less busy?'

'Of course, I'll come to your house tomorrow.'

'Good, I'll expect you.'

Kike was hardly able to sleep all night. She kept on thinking of various patterns she could do on people's hair. Next morning, she headed for Mama Berta's house.

'I know the style I want to do for you,' she announced as she came through the door.

'Have something to eat first, my child.'

'No thanks, I am okay for now; let's just get on with it.'

'If you say so,' agreed her hostess.

Kike began to section Mama Berta's hair.

She first divided the hair into eight straight lines from the front hair line to the nape of the neck. Then she wove the hair, following the lines she had sectioned. When she had finished, she examined the hair and told Mama Berta to look at it in a mirror. Her friend dashed to her room to look for an old mirror that her father had given her some years back. She gasped as she looked at the beautiful rows of extraordinary weaves on her hair.

'How very clever!' she exclaimed. 'They do resemble rows of corn,' she chirped happily.

'What did you say?' Kike was anxious to catch every word.

Mama Berta repeated herself, slowly signing at the same time.

'That's it,' shouted Kike.

'That's what?'

'Cornrow! I have been thinking of a name for this type of plaiting. It is very different from single plaits, I think cornrow is what best describes it. From today onwards, I'll call my new invention Cornrow.'

'God bless you, dear,' said Mama Berta, 'and may He also bless the work of your hands. Mark my words; for I have the gift of prophesy. This new discovery of yours will go places. People will come from far and near to have their hair adorned in beautiful plaits and your name will forever be a household name all over the world, as the originator of this special style. For your ashes, God will give unto you beauty, and for your shame, he will give you favour. All the years that the canker-worm has eaten will be restored to you many times over.'

Kike did not understand what Mama Berta was saying, but she sensed she was being prayed for so she said, 'Amen. I am happy you like your hair. I'll do another style for you when this gets untidy. What I need to start working on now is various scalp patterns. I don't want to limit my cornrows to straight front to back lines.'

'Do you want something to eat now?' her hostess offered.

'No, thank you, I must go home now.'

'Thanks once again, my child and give my love to your mother.'

Anyone would have thought Kike was drunk because of the way she was swaying from side to side and singing so loudly. Her mother was waiting for her by the door, slightly worried that she was late.

When Kike had eaten and rested, she told her parents about her exciting day. 'My new discovery will be called Cornrow,' she announced.

'Cornrow, why Cornrow?' asked her father.

'Because the finished style looks like rows of corn on the cob,' said Aduni, pointing to the hair that her daughter had plaited for her.

'Of course,' said Jakobu. 'Well done, I am really proud of you.'

As Aduni cooked dinner that night, she couldn't help smiling as she played back those happy thoughts. She had accepted the fact that her daughter might never hear again, but she was thankful for the support of her friends, especially Mama Berta. 'I feel I am now ready to face the challenge of nurturing my child through adolescence,' she mumbled.

Just then, Kike's cheery voice interrupted Aduni's thoughts. 'Mother, I am home,'

Aduni came in from the back yard to give her daughter a hug. She then gently instructed her to get the lanterns out and clean them.

'When you finish, light one of them and bring it to the back yard for me, it is now getting dark and I need to start serving the food.'

'What are we eating?' Kike asked.

'Moinmoin.'

'Oh, Mother, thanks. I love those steamed beans you make, I could eat a full pot and still want more.'

Aduni smiled. 'You won't want to do that or better still, I won't allow you to, because my belly cannot tolerate the horrible smelly fart that results from eating food made with beans.'

Jakobu laughed heartily at Aduni's jokes even though Kike could not hear, because her mum had turned her back to her, as she headed for the kitchen to finish off her cooking.

After dinner, Jakobu asked his daughter how her shop-hunting had been.

'Thank you, Father, the only shop that hasn't been rented out is this small place, close to Iya's stall.' Iya was Yomi's first wife and she had a teeny stand in the market where she sold salt. 'The owner is willing to lease it at a very cheap rate. I would like you and mother to go and see the place tomorrow, but I'd be happy to open the place to customers as soon as possible. I am positive that I'll be successful. All I need is to do nice styles on a couple of ladies and I'll soon have their friends, sisters and in-laws wanting to do their hair as well. Word of mouth is a very powerful advertising tool.'

Both mother and father sat speechless as their daughter unfolded her marketing strategy. It was Jakobu who broke the silence.

'Well, we are happy for you, child, and just before you came in, your mother and I talked about you and we are happy to give you our full support, isn't that right, Aduni?'

Aduni nodded in agreement.

When they had cleared up the dishes, Aduni, who was still excited about the prospect of her daughter plaiting hair for the chief's wife, came to sit beside her husband and placed her head lovingly on his chest.

'Shall we tell her then?' she asked.

'Tell who what?'

'Tell Kike about the message sent from Olori Teju. Surely you haven't forgotten.' Her eyes were twinkling with exhilaration.

'Oh that, I almost forgot. Yes, I think we should, but try and do the signs slowly so she can understand you,' said Jakobu considerately.

'Kike is now very good at lip-reading so I don't think I will strain myself much,' Aduni reassured her husband.

Then she got up and went round to where her daughter sat. She wanted to sit directly opposite her.

'Kike, we have some good news for you,' she began, pausing to see her daughter's reaction or at least know that she understood her. 'The chief's wife sent a message that she would like you to do her hair. I think she wants this new design of yours, em, what did you call it?'

'Cornrow,' said Jakobu proudly.

'Yes, Cornrow. Would you be happy to do it for her?'

Kike absorbed the information her mum was giving her; she understood it perfectly but she gave no response. She was deep in thought.

How did the chief's wife know about my new invention? Why would she want me, a deaf girl, shunned by everyone in the village, to do her hair? She is the chief's wife and she has her maids of honour who groom her every day. What does she have up her sleeves? she wondered.

'Kike!' Aduni called. 'Do you understand what I said?'

'Yes, Mother, I am just thinking, why does she want me to do her hair, when she has all her maids to groom her? Besides, what if I don't do the hair properly and she doesn't like it? You know Olori Teju and her vanity. She is a beautiful woman and she is ever dressing flamboyantly.'

Aduni smiled as she looked into her daughter's bright, honest brown eyes. Anyone could see that Kike was her pride and joy.

'My angel,' she said, putting her hands round her daughter after a long pause. 'I know you feel a bit inadequate right now, but you have nothing to fear. She was the one who came to you, not the other way round. I know you can do a beautiful job for her. You can practice more with my hair before you do hers, but I am confident you'll be fine. One thing I know for sure is that you always excel in anything you lay your hands on, isn't that right, Jakobu?' Aduni winked at Jakobu who had been quiet all along.

'Yes, yes, you can do it, Kike. Just go for it,' her father reassured her.

'Thanks, Father, and you, Mother, but I'd like to sleep on it. I'll see how I feel tomorrow.'

With that she said goodnight to her parents and went to her room. Kike's mind wandered a bit before sleep eventually came. She remembered the beautiful verse:

"I have more understanding than all my teachers:
For your testimonies are my meditations."

Psalm 119, verse 99.

She recalled what her friend, Mama Berta, had said, when she asked her for an interpretation of the psalm. Mama Berta had told her that it meant she would have more understanding of her work, even more than those who taught her, as long as she prays and meditates on the word of God, which is written in the Bible.

'Can you not see how true the verse is?' said Mama Berta, a strong believer in the power of words. 'Look at your new cornrow design for example, isn't it obvious that you now have more understanding than I, your tutor. Your new discovery is far more sophisticated in terms of skill and splendour.'

Chapter 11

INAUNDATED!

'KINDLY pass me that comb,' Kike called to one of the trainees standing nearby. It was a busy day and four people were still waiting impatiently to have their hair done. To make matters worse, Kike's salon was so tiny. It was built with wood and roofed with raffia and it had a small bench in one corner, where the client whose hair she was braiding sat. One assistant stood nearby to help as well as learn how to plait. There were three other clients, but due to lack of space, they had to sit on another bench outside the salon.

The young lady who was having her hair done was getting married in a few days and she had travelled all the way from Akinla, which was about 10 miles from Aje. She got to know about Kike through her friends, who had attended a women's meeting in Aje. The style worn by the chief's wife at the meeting was the talk of the village, and since then, Kike had been inundated with work. Nearly all the women in the village wanted their hair cornrowed and Kike's fame began to spread like wildfire.

Whenever people came together to gossip, her name was sure to be mentioned. People still found it incredulous that a deaf girl could make headway in life.

'Look at Kike. She cannot even hear herself speak, yet she has become successful by refusing to let her condition dictate her destiny,' a woman commented, a few days after she opened her salon.

As for the salon, it was always jam-packed. Kike also scored high marks in customer care. She treated each client with respect and she showed genuine interest in their welfare.

'Did you say you travelled from Akinla?' Kike asked the lady whose hair she was plaiting, trying to make conversation.

'Yes, I did, and I set out after the first cock crowed this morning. A woman would do anything for beauty,' she added, and everyone fell about laughing. Kike didn't respond, because she couldn't watch her client's mouth to lip-read her. However, she sensed the woman had made a funny remark because everyone was amused.

'Are you looking forward to your big day then?' the woman assisting Kike asked the bride-to-be.

'Yes I am; and I pray everything goes well on the day. Our cloths are made, palm wine has been ordered and my parents have invited Ayandeji to entertain.'

'Ayandeji! you mean Ayandeji will be at your wedding?' asked Kike's trainee. 'You must be from a prominent family, because that griot only performs for dignitaries and celebrities.'

'Well, my aunt is married to our village chief'

'That must be the reason,' said the trainee. 'Ayandeji is such a popular and talented man, known all over this region. My father used to drum with his band, and he came to our house once when I was a little girl. He is such a nice kind and humble man, but you see, everyone wants to have him at their ceremony, hence he is very busy. He can only do so much. If he is not careful, he'll die before his time. Perhaps, that is why he turns down many invitations. It is sad that people get offended, and say many horrible things about him.'

'Is it true that his wife ran away with one of his friends?' asked another customer.

'Unfortunately yes,' replied the trainee.

'That is really sad. How did he cope with the shame?'

'Well, he braced it and married another wife. In fact I heard that by the time his estranged wife came back for the rest of her things, just a month after she left, she met another woman living with him.'

'Men! Some of them have gone round more women than the number of clothes in their closet,' one of the women sitting outside commented and hissed indignantly. The laughter that ensued was deafening. The woman's husband had nine wives and uncountable concubines. The man was said to have lost count of the number of children he had, or that his women claimed were his.

Kike wondered what they were all talking about. She tried to lip-read some of them but she was getting too distracted, which slowed her work down, so she decided to concentrate on her work. It is better this woman gets her hair beautifully adorned for her wedding day, she thought.

At last she finished and after adding a few beads to enhance the beauty of the hair, she gave the woman a mirror to admire it.

'This is perfect,' said her client in appreciation. 'Thank you very much. I will be the first to wear cornrow plaits in my village.'

'And what are you going to call this style?' asked one of the women.

The young bride-to-be thought long and hard and said, 'I'll call it *Koju soko*, which means "turn and face your man".'

Everyone chortled and clapped loudly.

The young woman paid Kike and said goodbye.

'God's blessings on your wedding day,' Kike called after her.

'Amen, and may your work and fame continue to go before you,' the lady responded.

Since that day, young brides have continued to wear the style *Kojusoko*.

As for Kike, the more hair she did, the better she became. Sometimes, she could not meet the demand for her work and people had to wait for many hours. On one occasion, a woman waited a whole day and she still had to come back the following day before she could have her hair done.

Another problem arose. The salon was no longer adequate. People sat in long rows outside it and sometimes they occupied spaces that belonged to other traders and this was beginning to cause friction between Kike and her neighbours in the market. That was when she realised something had to be done fast.

She went to see her trusted friend Mama Berta on a Wednesday night. She finished early so that she could attend the weekly storytelling meeting held in her house. She hadn't missed any since her graduation.

That day, the topic for discussion was: *'A house set upon a hill cannot be hidden.'* The discussion was based on how people can release their hidden potential.

About thirty people attended, both men and women. Mama Berta now used her front yard, because her sitting-room was getting too small for the group.

During the question and answer period, a young woman asked how she could identify her talent.

'What is it that you mostly enjoy doing?' asked Mama Berta.

'Quite a number of things,' the young woman admitted.

'Yes, but what is it that you are known to be good at, or that family and friends have applauded you for in the past? That thing will stand out as you replay the compliments or comments you received and how proud you felt,' said their hostess, whose life was dedicated to helping people reach their full potential.

The woman squinted and a frown creased her brows as she thought long and hard for an answer to these questions.

'I know,' she said, raising her hand in a funny way. 'I enjoy cooking *amala* and *gbegiri* soup.' This is a Yoruba delicacy. Amala is made from yam powder and is best enjoyed with *gbegiri* - a type of bean soup.

Thunderous laughter followed.

The young woman became embarrassed. She quickly sat back on her chair, cowering like a frightened cat.

Even Mama Berta could not help laughing but she quickly got herself together and said, 'Oh no, don't be shy. That was a good and honest answer and I don't think we should take lightly what is important to other people. My child,' she continued, 'if cooking amala and gbegiri soup is what you enjoy doing, and if you know you've been ministering to people through your cooking, why not think of how to work on it, so that yours will be the best amala in this region?'

People began to roar with laughter again.

This time, Mama Berta sternly put a stop to it. 'I did not mean that as a joke, I want everyone to remember an old proverb that says, "A person's palm does not deceive him." I want you all to realise that what will make you prosper is right there in your hands. Have you not heard the quote: "God has chosen the foolish things of the world to confound the wise"?' She then turned to the woman again and said, 'Go in peace and work on your talent. I know that you will prosper in whatever you choose to do.'

And so it was that this young woman established a catering business exactly four months after this incident and the only food sold there was amala and gbegiri soup. Before long, she was managing a staff of four trained cooks who worked under her close supervision. Her canteen was right at the village centre, near the market, hence the place was always full.

That day, after everyone had left, Mama Berta and Kike had a tête-à-tête.

'You look stunning as always, my girl.' Mama Berta could not help giving a flattering remark to the handsome eighteen-year-old sitting in front of her. A good 5ft.8, Kike did not lack the gait that drew attention to her elegance. Her long neck was always held straight, which gave her the look of a female giraffe, showing off her beauty to onlookers. She was an embodiment of beauty and whenever she spoke, her white teeth flashed like the sparkle of diamonds when in contact with the sun. When she smiled, dimples graced each side of her cheeks, and any time she laughed, her voice rose and fell rhythmically.

'My word, every time I look at you, I see Aduni as a young woman. You are every inch like your mum except for your height, of course.'

Kike was able to grasp all that her friend said, so she smiled shyly and said, 'Thank you, ma, you are also very beautiful.'

'Nonsense, I am growing old now, but thanks for the compliment all the same. Now, how is business?'

'Very well, thank you.'

'You look tired - have you been working too hard?'

Kike merely nodded.

'Poor girl, I'll get you something to eat.' Mama Berta immediately went to her kitchen and soon came back with a plate of roasted plantain and cool water for her guest. Kike, who was hungry, began to munch away.

'I came by your salon yesterday morning,' Mama Berta said after a while. When she got no response, she stood up to bring one of her oil lamps closer to where they sat so that Kike could lip-read her. 'I said I came by your salon yesterday,' she repeated.

'Really? I didn't see you, I am sorry.'

'I know. I didn't want to disturb you so I crept quietly away, as you were really busy.'

Yes, that's one of the things that I want to discuss with you.'

'Why, what's happened?'

'Nothing serious, it's just that the shop is far too small for me now and the work is expanding rapidly. I don't know what to do. Also, the demand for hair braiding is becoming more than I can manage alone. Honestly, I never envisaged it getting to this.'

'You sound a bit downcast,' the elder observed. 'This is success knocking at your door. I would have thought you'd be excited.'

'What happens if I can't cope?' asked Kike with a frown. 'Last week, a woman had to wait two days before she could have her hair done. Today, I had to send some clients away because I won't be able to do their hair until next week and some have been waiting since Monday.'

'There is always a way out of every problem. This is a challenge,' said Mama Berta, trying frantically to explain every phrase to her deaf friend. 'Have you thought of training more people to work for you?'

'Yes,' said Kike. 'The thing is I haven't concentrated on training them properly. They only observe what I do, and that is not enough for them to learn the art. They need to practise. Unfortunately, all the clients want *me* to do their hair.'

'Aha! There you go; a step in the right direction. How about spending half a day each week focusing on training your workers, and any client who comes in at that time pays half the fee, if they are prepared to allow your trainees to do their hair. However, these trainees must have practised on their siblings or neighbours, and you need to see their work and sanction it as good even if not perfect, before you allow them to do your customers' hair.'

Kike nodded each time she understood what her friend said.

'Don't take on too many trainees as you are just starting out yourself. Find two good and honest girls who won't use you and abandon you. Train them well and once they begin to show signs of mastering the skill, employ them.'

'Where will I get such good people?' Kike asked.

'Pray and God will help you to choose the best. Ask for the spirit of wisdom and understanding, just like King Solomon of old. As for the problem of your salon being too small, let's not discuss that tonight. Come and see me next Saturday.'

Kike left her mentor's house that night a happy woman. It was as if a heavy burden was lifted off her shoulders.

Chapter 12

THE HOUSE ON A HILL

IT was early Saturday morning. The cockerels were just starting their glorious concert. Kike felt very tired. It must be the busy week I had, she thought as she rolled back and forth on her mat. Suddenly she remembered her appointment with Mama Berta, so she jumped up and quickly went to have a wash.

'Mother!' she called, as she made her way to the bathroom.

'I am here, precious,' Aduni answered from the kitchen where she was busy cooking breakfast.

'Do you remember we are going together to see Mama Berta?'

'Yes, I do. We'll set out once we've eaten.'

Later that morning, they arrived at Mama Berta's, only to discover she wasn't in. She had gone to the chief's house to discuss the possibility of renting one of his properties for Kike. Mama Berta knew it wasn't going to be easy to convince the chief to let out his property, but she was prepared to do her best.

'Sir, that house is just sitting there rotting away. You are blessed with so many; why not release this one to Kike? It will make a lot of difference to her business. You see, I have offered to build her a small salon on my land, but she wouldn't hear of it. I quite understand, because Kike is a proud and independent-minded girl, and she already feels she owes me a lot. I can identify with her in that I don't like being at people's mercy either. It gives me a sense of achievement to know I am able to fend for myself.

'But the house on a hill is a valuable treasure,' the chief argued. 'It was bequeathed to me by my grandmother, and I am not ready to part with it. By the way, why do you want that particular house?'

'Because it's ideal,' explained Mama Berta. 'It is well located, and it is close to the village border. Kike has clients that come from neighbouring towns and villages; these people will be able to locate her salon easily.'

Mama Berta knew the chief well enough. He was not one to part with any of his earthly possessions just like that, and he was well known for his stinginess. In spite of this, she was not going to take no for an answer.

'Your Highness,' she continued, 'I will pay you a rent for that house until Kike is well established in her business. How about that?'

The chief thought long and hard. 'Let me think about it, Berta,' he said at last. 'Come back in two weeks and I'll give you my answer.'

'Your Highness, I am not leaving your presence today until you give me an answer; yes or no. I am not being rude, but Kike and her mother are waiting for me in my house as we speak. I did not envisage that I would have such trouble in convincing you to be generous to a poor deaf girl who has broken all records in the history of our land. She has swum against the tide and is fulfilling her destiny in spite of all the odds against her. Many people with such disabilities are on street corners begging for alms but she has brought honour both to her family and to this village. I thought the least you could do is support her as she continues to stretch herself to reach her full potential.'

She paused to allow the chief time to digest all she'd been saying. After a while she continued her emotional plea. 'Many in this village know you for your compassion. Have you forgotten how you came to Ladoye's rescue when he was about to be ostracised because of his deformity? You sent him to one of your friends in Ota village and he was well taken care of. Please do this favour for Kike and your name will be recorded in history as a kind and generous chief.'

Mama Berta could see from the corner of her eyes that the chief was starting to feel good about himself, because he was beginning to nod at every statement she made. Suddenly, the chief sat up on his chair and said,

'All right, you win.'

'What!' Mama Berta exclaimed, hardly believing her luck.

'I said you win.'

'Sir, you mean you agree to rent out the house?'

'Yes, but on one condition – that house must be kept immaculately clean always and if at any time I find it not well kept I will evict Kike – I promise you that.'

'Many thanks, your highness,' said Mama Berta as she bowed in courtesy to the chief. 'You are most gracious. When can she start using the place?'

'As soon as I receive my first rent,' the chief said unashamedly.

'Very well, I'll bring you the first rent tomorrow and I will help Kike tidy the place up for next week.'

With that she hurried out of the chief's presence before he changed his mind.

Meanwhile, Aduni and her daughter were still waiting patiently for Mama Berta, not knowing what was going on in the chief's house. It was getting too hot indoors so both of them came outside for fresh air. Just then, they saw their friend coming into the compound and they hurried towards her. They exchanged greetings and Mama Berta went straight to the point.

'Listen, I have some good news for both of you. Let's go indoors.' When they were all seated, she narrated to them how she had bargained with the chief for the 'house on a hill' for Kike's use. She tried her best to slow down in spite of her excitement, so that Kike could follow what she was saying.

'You mean that beautiful house close to the village border would be available to my daughter?' asked Aduni. Both mother and daughter were knocked for six. They were not expecting that kind of miracle.

'Yes, 'the house on a hill' is now available for rent and the first tenant is Kike. It is a very beautiful house, but like I always say, only the best is fit for the child of a king, and Kike is a child of God, the king of heaven and earth,

157

so she deserves the very best.' Then she turned to Kike and said, 'now child, please let me pay your rent until you are well established.'

'Oh no, I think I earn enough to be able to pay the rent,' Kike protested. 'You have done more than enough for me already. I owe you so much.'

'You do not owe me anything, dear. Where would I take all my chattels when I die? I believe I was richly blessed with all I have for a purpose, and that is to bless people around me. Of what use are my earthly possessions to me beyond the grave? I don't have any child that I can bestow anything on. You and a few others are all I have got. Please do not refuse my offer. At least let me help you for a few months.'

'I do appreciate your love,' said Kike thankfully. Although she did not grasp all her friend had just said, she sensed from her expression that she was eager to help. She also knew that saying no to Mama Berta was like rejecting her. She was a sensitive woman and she would feel offended.

Mama Berta was happy that Kike accepted her offer. 'That's settled then,' she said joyfully, 'I think we should all go there some time next week and get the place ready.'

Two weeks later, Kike moved into her new salon. The house was the only one on the hill, where it was located, hence its name, 'house on a hill.' It was built on a land of about one acre. Although it was an old house, it looked stunning with its square shape and flat roof. The wall was built with red clay and the outside wall was decorated with stunning colourful stones that glittered in the sun.

The house had four rooms in total, two large ones and two smaller ones. The room closest to the main entrance was the largest and this was to be the main salon. The second largest room would be used as storage, while one of the smaller rooms would be used as kitchen cum staff room, where Kike's workers could sit down to rest when they needed to take a break

'This is just perfect,' said Kike as she hung the new wall carving that her father gave her the day before, as a present. She went outside to examine the view at the rear of the house. It was breathtaking! She could see the entire village sprawled out at the bottom of the hill. The air was cool and fresh and the smell of mango filled the air. There were two mango trees in the orchard, along with an orange tree and a banana tree.

Within a few days, it was back to business as usual. Most of the clients that came to have their hair cornrowed were young girls. It wasn't that the older generation did not avail themselves of the trendy hairstyles, but Cornrow was a fashion embraced mostly by teenagers and young adults.

The salon soon became as busy as a beehive. Kike decided to get permission from the chief to build a tent outside the house, for clients who needed fresh air while they waited. The tent was meant to protect them from the scourging sun.

The chief sent one of his trusted workers, Femi, to build the tent for Kike.

'Peace be unto this house,' Femi greeted when he got to the salon.

'And to the visitor,' answered one of the braiders. 'Oh, it's you Femi, please come in and have a seat and I'll fetch Kike. She is in the orchard, picking ripe mangoes.'

Before long, Kike came indoors. 'Thanks for coming,' she said to Femi. Please come with me to the kitchen; the salon is a bit busy this morning. When they got to the kitchen, Femi said, 'The chief told me you needed a tent, where would you like me to build it?'

Kike didn't answer because, for some reason she was unable to maintain eye contact with the young man. All along she looked away.

Femi moved closer to Kike and held her hands

Kike's heart began to race, as she felt his hands on hers.

This was the man she'd been day-dreaming about for the past six months, ever since she first set eyes on him at the chief's party.

Their meeting had been a dramatic one. The chief had invited Kike and her parents to a party, to celebrate his tenth year as the village chief. As Kike sat with other guests, she felt as if someone was peering at her. She always had this strange feeling whenever anyone stared at her. She turned round to see the most handsome man she had ever laid her eyes on, sitting alone under the shade of an odan tree. He was about twenty-two years old, and he gaped at her, not in a rude way, but lovingly with dazzling eyes.

Kike's heart began to race very fast and she quickly turned round to face her food. For the rest of the evening, she continued to cast occasional glances at this strange man but their eyes met each time she looked.

'Wow, could this be an admirer?' she wondered. 'Who is he anyway? I haven't seen him around here before.'

159

She didn't have to wonder for long because just then the chief stood up to give a vote of thanks to his guests and before he sat down he said, '...and now, I would like to introduce a talented young man to you all. His name is Femi, and he came all the way from Omi Adio village to work alongside the builders who are constructing my new house. He specialises both in wood-carving and masonry and he would be responsible for the craftwork that would make the house look magnificent. My selfish prayer is that one of our village beauties would tempt him to stay in our village, Aje.'

At this last statement, the villagers began to laugh and some of them clapped their hands loudly as the chief beckoned to Femi to join him, where he was sitting.

Femi was a shy man and everyone could see how uncomfortable he was. He kept on smiling as the villagers acknowledged his presence. They waved at him and some, who were close enough, patted his back.

Kike asked her mum what the excitement was all about, and her mum tried as much as she could to explain things to her.

Later the party ended and everyone went home. However, Kike couldn't sleep. She kept seeing Femi's face all through the night. She tossed around on her bed visualising the handsome six-foot lad.

One Sunday morning, Kike went for Sunday service at the village hall. The church was established by Mama Berta, shortly after her graduation a few years back and one of Mama Berta's converts was the pastor. Initially, there were only seventeen people: six men and eleven women. Now it had about forty regular attendees, including little children.

During the service, Kike began to have this eerie feeling again that someone was looking at her, so she looked around to see who it was.

Ah! It's him again, Femi. He was sitting on the same row as she was, only four chairs away. Her heart was now beating so fast she thought the woman sitting next to her could hear it.

Femi winked at her and she smiled back.

After the service, he quickly came over to where she sat and shook her hands. He had been doing some research on Kike, so he already knew she was deaf.

He spoke slowly and gesticulated all along. 'How are you, and how is work?' he asked politely.

'Very well, thank you, and how is your work?' Kike asked, stumbling through her words.

'I am doing what I can at the moment. I haven't quite settled in yet.'

'When are you going back to your village?' Kike asked anxiously.

'I don't know yet,' Femi answered, to her relief. 'Can I walk you home?'

'Em...yes please,' said Kike.

Both of them went to greet the pastor and Mama Berta before leaving.

'I'm going home now but I'll see you on Wednesday,' said Kike to the elder.

'Looking forward to it,' Mama Berta answered. Then she winked at Kike when no one was looking.

Cheeky, thought Kike, smiling. Why was she winking at me like that? Maybe it is because of Femi. I know she will be on my case on Wednesday and I will play her up.

On the way, Kike asked Femi the question that had plagued her all day. 'Are you a Christian?'

'Well, I wasn't before I came to Aje, but the family I am staying with at the moment are, and they told me some wonderful stories about the religion. Many of which I have never heard of. I was eager to know more so I have arranged to see Mama Berta, who I hear is your dear friend.'

'Yes,' said Kike. 'She is more than a friend, she is my angel.'

There was so much Femi wanted to ask Kike, so much he wanted to share with her, but he knew he had to be calm and play his cards right. He had befriended a number of women in the past, but it had always been for the fun of it. He had never felt this way about any girl and he was determined to woo the young maiden.

Kike didn't want Femi to come into the house with her, so as they came closer to her house she said, 'Thank you for walking me home.'

Femi got the message and quickly said, 'Please don't thank me – it was a pleasure. Can I see you again soon?'

'Yes, next week in church,' she answered, choosing her words with care.

Kike had always dreamt of a man who would sweep her off her feet, love her and marry her. She, however, was determined that anyone who would marry her must love her for who she was; hence she was not prepared to lead Femi on. 'I want it to happen naturally. I want to be wooed. No matter what, I will never throw myself at any man,' she always told her friend Mama Berta.

'Can I not see you before then?' Femi pleaded.

'I am very busy with my work all week. The only day I have is Sunday.'

'Okay, see you on Sunday.'

Kike could see the disappointed look on his face. 'Bye for now,' she said and hurried away.

Luckily for Femi, on Tuesday of the same week, the chief sent for him, and told him to go and build a tent for Kike. Femi did not waste time; he went to Kike's salon that same day, because it was an opportunity to see the woman of his dreams.

'I was told you need a tent,' Femi repeated when he got Kike's attention.

'Yes, can you build one right there on the grass,' she replied, pointing to where she wanted it.

'Very well, I'll start immediately.'

'Let me know if you need anything,' Kike mumbled as she went back to resume her work.

At lunchtime she asked one of her workers to set a table for her and Femi in the front yard.

Strangely, before they began to eat, Femi came over to where Kike sat and held her hands. He then asked her to look at him directly in the eye, and when he knew he had her full attention, he said, 'Kike, I want you to be my wife and mother of my children.' Femi had rehearsed this proposal all week. He had planned it for the following Sunday, but thanks to the chief, the opportunity came earlier than he intended.

Kike was taken by surprise when she eventually grasped what Femi said. She jumped off her seat, but unfortunately she slipped. Femi panicked and dived for her but he was too late. Before he got to her she had hit the concrete floor, landing heavily on her right arm.

He immediately lifted her and carried her in his strong arms as if she was a ten-year-old girl. 'Are you all right?' he asked.

Still in shock, Kike shouted, 'Put me down!' and she struggled to free herself. This drew the attention of her workers and clients. They thought something was wrong and they all rushed out of the salon to see what it was.

The scene that met their eyes was most embarrassing. There was their boss in the arms of the handsome young man who had come to build a tent for them.

They did not know what to say. One of them quickly excused herself and ran back indoors and others did the same, except an elderly woman whose turn it was to have her hair done after their lunch break. She stayed back to see what was really happening.

'Are you okay, my child?' she signed to Kike when she heard her whining in pain.

'I think so,' Kike answered. 'I fell off my chair and hurt my arm and this kind man is just helping me up.'

The old lady came over to where she was. 'Let me see your arm,' she said. 'Thank God it was not a bad fall. Just some bruises, that's all. I'll get a flannel and water to clean it up for you.' When the woman had gone indoors, Femi, who was shaken by the whole event, used the opportunity to apologise to Kike.

'I am so sorry,' he said, looking very embarrassed.

Kike said, 'Don't worry; it's not your fault. I am sure I'll be fine.' Then she looked up, and to her amazement Femi had tears in his eyes. She fixed her gaze on him to be certain she wasn't imagining things.

She wanted to say something, but choked on her words. She simply sat there staring at him. She had never seen a man cry before. In her village, men knew how to hide their feelings; it came with practice. She had always thought many of them were like emotional zombies. Many parents saw to it that their sons suppressed their feelings, from when they were very young.

'You can't cry; you're a man! A man must never be soft and must never show his emotions or people will think he is weak,' parents would say to their male offspring.

That was why Kike was deeply touched to see Femi in tears. How could a man so strong and so masculine be so soft-hearted? she wondered. It didn't add up. This must be the sign I asked for, she thought as she looked into his eyes. I have prayed for a sign to help me know the man I'll marry. I prayed that the man would do something out of the ordinary that'll touch my heart.

Then she leaned towards Femi, and whispered in his ear. 'I will be your wife and mother of your children,' but before Femi could say anything, she hurried indoors.

Kike was on cloud nine for the rest of the day.

Femi continued to build the tent until Kike was ready to close the salon for the day.

When everyone had left, both of them sat down on a bench outside the house and talked till it was too dark for Kike to either lip-read Femi or see his gesticulations.

'We'd better be going or my parents will send out a search party for me,' said Kike jokingly.

'I want to stay here with you forever,' Femi replied, stroking her long hair.

That night as they descended the hill back to the village, Femi gently stretched out his right hand and held Kike's left hand, squeezing it firmly but gently, as if to say, 'I will never leave you nor forsake you.' Kike's heart picked up the message instantly and though no words were said, she knew deep within her that she had found the man of her dreams.

Chapter 13

KIKE THE LEGEND

IT was exactly two years since Kike moved to 'the house on a hill.' She now had three women working for her full time. They were talented and hardworking and Kike gave them a good salary, because without them she couldn't have coped with the workload.

In spite of this, Kike still found it difficult to keep up with demand. Many people came from places as far as Ota, twenty miles away from Aje. Those who came from such faraway places always had to sleep over in the village.

It was not only her talent that drew the crowd. It was also her story, her personality and above all, her faith in God. She shared her faith with her clients and she was always a source of encouragement to both young and old.

Kike now had regular styles that she plaited on her clients. The most popular ones were *Koroba* (bucket), *Ipako elede* (occipital of a pig), *Aja n'loso* (stooping dog),

Koju soko (face your man) and a host of others too numerous to mention. Each pattern told a story because Kike sectioned the hair so that the finished style looked exactly like its name. People could not but wonder at the skill required to design some of the complicated ones.

Some clients presented Kike with challenges. For example, a woman came to her house one Sunday afternoon and said she'd been sent as an 'ambassador of peace' to a family torn apart by feud. She was going to speak to the head of the clan and she wanted Kike to weave a pattern for her that symbolised peace. She wanted to use her hairstyle as a good-luck charm so that she'd be well received and listened to. She booked to do her hair the following Thursday, which would give Kike plenty of time to think about a style for her.

Almost immediately, Kike began to use her imagination. First she thought of where she would go if she needed peace and tranquillity. The first thought that came to her mind was the river. Yes, that was a good place to find peace, but how do I design water on a person's hair? she wondered.

Time was drawing closer for this client's appointment and Kike hadn't come up with anything. On Wednesday evening, she and Femi took a walk to a brook near her house and Kike shared her dilemma with her lover. Unfortunately he couldn't help, but he listened to her.

They sat down for a while by the brook and Femi began to throw pebbles into the stream. As he did so, a ripple emerged, which grew and spread until another pebble was thrown. Kike joined Femi in throwing pebbles into the water and she watched the ripples as they formed and disappeared.

Then, as if struck by a thunderbolt, she yelled, 'That's it!'

'That's what?' Femi queried.

'Ripples,' she shouted, pointing at the brook.

'Yes, I know, but what has that got to do with anything?' Femi looked befuddled.

'I am going to weave ripples on my client's hair tomorrow.'

'What! You mean you can actually create the shape I am looking at in that river on someone's hair?'

'I think I can, I'll try,' Kike answered quietly, starting to doubt herself.

'No, don't be discouraged – I wasn't trying to make you feel inadequate, I am just full of awe at your creative mind and abilities,' said Femi, reassuringly.

'Please throw a pebble into the water again,' Kike requested.

Femi did, and this time, Kike watched the ripple effect closely and said, 'Thank you, problem solved.'

Later that evening, she worked on how she would section the style on her client whose appointment was the following morning.

The woman came in early the next day, and Kike did the ripple effect pattern on her hair. It was a simple style but the sectioning was done in such a way that no one could tell where the braiding started or ended. Everyone present in the salon that day was amazed. The pattern, though simple, was very delicate and beautiful.

The client saw the admiring look on the faces of the ladies there and said, 'I can only guess that Kike has performed a braid miracle again.'

Everyone laughed.

Then she turned to Kike and said slowly, 'What is the name of this style?'

Kike swiftly passed her a mirror before answering; 'The style you're now wearing is called "Ripple Effect" and I pray that Peace will go with you.'

Kike later heard that the woman was successful in her ambassadorial work and the family she went to see agreed to reconcile.

Before long, Kike opened a second salon and she trained four other women to work there regularly. Many months after that, she opened a new one at Akinla, one of the neighbouring villages. The woman who worked there was the bride on whose hair she first plaited the style, *koju soko*, some years back. This woman had come back for training after her wedding. When she had mastered the art, she begged Kike to open a branch in her village, so that she could run it. Kike eventually agreed and she gave the woman her full support. Initially, she travelled once a month to help with the nitty-gritty of initial set-up, but she later handed over to the woman because the journey back and forth was getting too strenuous for her.

Before long, Kike's business expanded to six more villages and two towns in the region. Slowly and steadily, cornrow became a well known method of hair braiding in sub-Saharan Africa.

As for Kike, public speaking became a regular part of her work. Nearly every week, she was invited to attend one meeting or another as a motivational speaker, not only in her village but also in the neighbouring villages. Such meetings were always packed. Initially, Jakobu went with her to these meetings but Femi took over from him after his engagement to Kike.

Femi was always there for her, no matter how busy he was. The chief gave them a piece of land, and he worked extremely hard with some of the village builders to build their house on it. However, whenever she needed to travel, he abandoned his work to go with her.

Kike knew she'd been blessed with Femi and she also took good care of him. Since the day she said 'yes' to him, he had ceased calling her Kike. He began to call her Wura, which means gold in Yoruba language.

'I have found the greatest treasure in the world,' Femi told his parents, when he went to bring them to Aje for the wedding. 'I have never been so happy in my life and I vow to make her happy all the rest of her life.'

His friends who came with him for the ceremony teased him throughout the journey. 'What did this woman give you to eat? Do you know that women in Aje village are reputed to mix love potion with their men's food so that they can worship the ground they walk on,' they laughed.

'Well, I am happy it was Kike's love potion I ate and no one else's,' Femi replied. When his friends realised they weren't going to succeed in making fun of him, they stopped their banter and instead asked sensible questions about how Femi's romance had bloomed. He in turn delighted his friends with a moving tale of love at first sight.

EPILOGUE

ONE hot Saturday afternoon, thirteen weeks after my grandma started the story of Kike; I went to her house, to have my hair plaited in preparation for school. I was excited as usual to hear the continuation of the narrative. Alas, I did not know that the story I'd enjoyed so much was about to end. As I sat down, Grandma looked at me sadly and said, 'Child, our story is gradually drawing to a close.'

'Oh no!'

'Yes, pet, all things, either good or bad, have a beginning and an end, but don't let that spoil your day. Let me round up the tale and I promise that from today onwards I'll start plaiting some of Kike's original styles for you, and also tell you the stories that inspired each of the patterns.'

My eyes lit up at the prospect of this, and I told Grandma I was ready to hear the concluding part.

'That's my girl,' she said and continued: 'Kike eventually married Femi, her sweetheart, and their marriage was blessed with three lovely children. Femi was faithful to his words and he loved Kike and cared for her always.

'As for Kike's Cornrow invention, it spread all over the region of West Africa and throughout the continent of Africa as a whole. Later, due to migration of Africans to different parts of the world, the art soon travelled across the oceans, and today you can see men and women in Europe, America and other places, wearing some of her original designs.

'Kike's dream of becoming a storyteller did come true, as she went from village to village and from town to town speaking to people, young and old, about her trials and triumphs, and also about her faith in God. She was a source of inspiration to many people.

'Life, however, is not without its sad moments. When Kike was pregnant with her second child, her aunt Bolaji, who inspired her to become a storyteller died peacefully in her sleep. An urgent message had been sent to Aduni to come to Ijohun because her sister, Bolaji was dying. Unfortunately, Aduni arrived too late; her beloved sister died four hours before she got there.

'It was a huge blow to Aduni and she cried herself to sleep nearly every night and was restless even in her sleep. Kike was heartbroken. Only six months before her aunt died, she had asked her mother to travel with her to Ijohun to see her, and her mother promised to go with her after she'd had the baby. None of them knew they would never see their beloved Bolaji again. That was why Kike's second child was named Bolaji after her late aunt.

'As for Mama Berta, she left the village to live closer to her relatives in Ibadan, which was about 100 miles from Aje. Her sisters and brothers wanted her to live closer to them so that they could look after her, as she was getting old. Kike later heard that she had established a church in Ibadan, and she still ran her workshops, with the help of two dedicated women whose lives had been touched by her kindness and love.'

At this point, Grandma paused and said, 'I have come to the end of the story. I hope you enjoyed it.'

'Yes,' I said, 'thank you for sharing it with me. You are an amazing storyteller and I would like to tell stories with such eloquence and vigour some day.'

'Thank you, my child,' Grandma replied to my compliments, and she continued to braid my hair. None of us said anything for the next forty-five minutes. In my mind, I was playing back this amazing story that had lasted thirteen weeks.

Grandma's voice pierced through my daydreaming. 'Today, the cornrow pattern I am plaiting for you is called Ripple Effect, in honour of Kike, the legendary weaver.

I was over the moon, because I knew the commotion that my hairstyle was going to cause in school the following week.

About the Author:

ABIMBOLA ALAO

A BIMBOLA Alao read classics at the University of Ibadan, Nigeria, where she obtained a BA (Hon.) in 1988 and a Masters degree in 1991. She presently works as an Educational Consultant and Professional Storyteller for Lampo Educational Services, which she set up 2001, shortly after she finished her teacher training program at the University of Plymouth, England.

Lampo Educational Services, which is based in Devon, aims to bring fun and creativity to learning through enriching cross-curricular services. This is done through interactive storytelling and music, using costumes, props and multicultural artefacts. This organisation also offers training workshops to teachers, storytellers, parents and carers.